MILLER HOMES

TRUTH OR FICTIONAL

CHARLES FEGGANS

Copyright © 2023 Charles Feggans.

All rights reserved. No part of this book may be reproduced, stored, or transmitted by any means—whether auditory, graphic, mechanical, or electronic—without written permission of both publisher and author, except in the case of brief excerpts used in critical articles and reviews. Unauthorized reproduction of any part of this work is illegal and is punishable by law.

ISBN: 979-8-89031-782-7 (sc)
ISBN: 979-8-89031-783-4 (hc)
ISBN: 979-8-89031-784-1 (e)

Because of the dynamic nature of the Internet, any web addresses or links contained in this book may have changed since publication and may no longer be valid. The views expressed in this work are solely those of the author and do not necessarily reflect the views of the publisher, and the publisher hereby disclaims any responsibility for them.

One Galleria Blvd., Suite 1900, Metairie, LA 70001
(504) 702-6708

Miller Homes
Truth or Fictonal

By

Charles Feggans
Based on a true story

Miller Homes was located on the east side of Trenton New Jersey. The activities in this story took place in and around Miller Homes. Miller Homes was aired on television's channel 6 ABC news and printed in the local newspapers. The Mayor at that time made a statement about how the troublesome area had become dangerous. People started changing the name Miller Homes to 'Killer Homes.' The Police Chief lost control of arresting criminals and such. People to this day are still talking about how Miller Homes went down and had to be destroyed.

CHAPTER One

Introduction to the Background

Reminiscing of the days of old, some folks can still remember when the majority of people living in cities were classified as white. These were mostly middle and upper class citizens who took pride in their row homes, making them an image to be found mainly in magazines. Streets and sidewalks were often cared for by residents who resided within their neighborhoods. When someone in the neighborhood wasn't sweeping a sidewalk or cleaning along the edge of a curb, a neatly clad uniformed city worker would come along pushing a rail handled 55-gallon drum mounted upon a set of large spoke wheels attached to a cart and armed with a long handle straw push broom and a scooping shovel was there to keep the area clean.

Most neighborhoods were always a matter of pride. Window-sills with small outside ledges were daily decorated with small pots of colorful blooming flowers, adding a highlight to the red contour two and three story brick faced building structures. Trees along the sidewalks drooped with an abundance of various shading tree leaves that danced to the lightly breeze, in turn, provided a portion of shade to the many homes.

Late night residents sat outdoors on porches sometimes until the wee hours of the morning unmolested, talking about events of the day's passing, while children played unattended in parks, playgrounds and along streets, which was an everyday and every night common thing.

Life during those days seemed to be grand for those living in the area. No one could have predicted that a new error of living was beginning to unfold. It seemed like over night non-white families began moving into the neighborhoods. The new arrives weren't as charismatic as the exiting residents and their descendent. The exiting residents took offense to being subjected to interracial neighborhoods and in massive groves, sold their homes to non-white buyers and quickly began moving to country-sides and townships where they could continue to live in, what they believed was, a segregated culture surrounded by beauty among their own nationalities.

At some point in time during this transition, many of the well kept properties took on the appearance of deterioration while the new residents enjoyed life more so than tending to their properties. The influx of new residents showed very little concern for the beauty that these homes once portrayed.

Many years passed before the new influx of inhabitance realized the down swing that their Community had fallen into and what had happened to their well kept neighborhoods. Facing their environment change, it had become a semi-ghetto. The community had succumbed to such a very bad appearance that one by one, homes were being abandon and boarded up. People at City Officials took notice of the area and ordered city workers to begin tearing down unsightly homes, leaving gaps between them which created junk yards. Piles of trash and rubbish began accumulating along streets which spilled over onto sidewalks, in yards, and along alleyways. Abandon cars, tireless with broken windows became a common everyday eye sore. Some of the concerned older residents had succumbed to a point where they could no longer go on living in this rundown environment. It was time for a change.

One evening, a small concerned group of residents met in one of the neighboring resident's home to come up with plans to bring back some of the beauty to their neighborhoods. The committee knew they would have to take a strong stand in order to lift up from this deteriorating environmental situation. They would have to band together to see that the clean up would not be taken lightly by neighbors throughout the neighborhoods.

Flyers were circulated throughout the neighborhoods, committee members talked with residents on their porch and at various locations throughout the neighborhoods calling for residents to support their efforts. The committee members were filled with much excitement as they spread the word pertaining to their future plans. The committee knew the residents could only do but so much. Outside help was needed, people with knowledge and most important, an ample amount of money, something they didn't have. However, after several weeks had passed and not being able to gain the support that was needed, the committee decided that their complaint for the neighborhoods clean up should be aired at City Hall. At the time, City Hall was known to have fixed up a number of other neighborhoods with conditions similar, if not worse than theirs. The committee felt that it was only right that every citizen had the right to a clean and healthy neighborhood environment. After all, they too were taxpaying members of this community. And the way their neighborhoods stood in its present condition, represented a bad reflection on the city's image as a whole. The committee came to a conclusion that if the homes could be restored in such a fashion as to add some beauty to the neighborhood, and the streets were rid of the abandoned vehicles, trash and eye sore items, there was the possibility of attracting a portion of the departed residents who had completely uprooted and moved away from the area into returning to their old neighborhood. But, after just one meeting with City Officials, the officials came together in a week long decision and unanimously decided that no amount of fixing up would rid the city of its plague of people who thrived on letting their property run down, but in reality, something had to be done. This was not the time to do so. The committee vow to stay on City's Officials back until some sort of plan was set in place.

Three years has passed. By this time, City Officials was able to come up with a created plan for this section of the city. The plans were to build what most people would call the promise land of new housing, MILLER HOMES.

Approximately a year later, the complex got underway on this eastern side of the city, within the area where the complaint had derived. Three years into construction, two-twenty story high-rise Towers and fifty single two story row home units were built. The landscape was cultivated within an illustrious grassy setting. An abundance of shade trees sprinkled throughout the area with an assortment of shrubs nestling close to the modern Towers and newly built row homes.

Many low income residents and committee members dream had come true. All the committee's hard work with City Officials had paid off and now they were pleased to receive a new start in a much nicer and clearer environment. Everyone who moved into Miller Homes vowed to do all that was possible to keep Miller Homes the pride of new achievements.

Twenty years has swept away sense the first day the new Tenants had moved into their apartment complex. Many of the first Tenants have long since moved on, leaving Miller Homes to fade from its lustrous image. The once pride of new developmental achievements, the colorful brick-faced single units and Towering buildings with its picturesque landscapes, now grossly marred with graffiti. Many pieces of windows frames hold jagged pieces of glass barely attached to their outlined frames. Some covered with plastic or cardboard resembling a historical forgotten site. In the mitts of scattered pieces of papers and wrappers, it is not hard to find trash rolling across the courtyards and driveways in the height of a mild stirring breeze. Most of the driveways in the height of a sunny day show reflections of broken glass imbedded into the asphalt as reminders of something that was once beautiful to the eye, now mixed with odd shapes of chalk marking designed for street games.

Fewer trees, mostly barren with multiple broken limbs and voids of most leaves, resemble tentacles that once held thriving plots of vegetation, now struggle to grow on branches high above a human's reach as they reach for the sky yet to be disturbed.

Children trample and play in seas of harden earth where grass was the admiration of visitors. The only grassy vegetation to remain in existence clung to the Towers' base just out of reach from people routinely creating paths and playing in the area.

A single, empty wine bottle stands on its neck with its back against the step to Tower One's entrance as a welcome sign for the many scattered pieces of liter that spread along the floors from one level to the next throughout the Towering building.

Within the interior of the Towers, a strong scent of urine, generated by the day's heat stretch beyond the entrance inward hovering close to the stairwells and in-lining hallways. Along the long hallways within the Towers, many light bulbs have been removed by Tenants who felt the establishment owed them something for whatever reason, leaving one or two fading lights to cast dimming glows throughout the entire floor level. Rodents and roaches move about freely making use of the lack of light to feed upon piles of trash and garbage within the confining structures.

Old and new creations of graffiti on stairways give rise to a new group of promising artist as it continuously winds up through the stairways and down the long halls into the partly fading, darkening areas.

On partly sunny days when the sun's light moves across the face of the Towers, a glimmer of light tunnels its way through the door less doorways leading into the lobbies.

It has been years since the Towers held front entrance doors. There is a saying among Tenants who believe, years ago, a band of men in work uniforms, ordered by City Officials, came through the Towers late one night and removed all the Towers main doors because of a shortage in construction budget at another work site. During that time, the Tenants became highly upset and made it a point to collectively visit City Official and demand the doors be return. During cold months, the missing doors gave the Towers a hollow look, but the worse aspect was focused on a tremendous draft to the apartments, leaving some Tenants sicken to near death from the still cold that lingered outside of each apartment's doorway.

A formal investigation was held by City Officials to locate the perpetrators who ran off with the doors. As part of the investigation, a group of City Officials went to Miller Homes to see first hand how the area had deteriorated. What they saw was totally beyond belief. After one visit, they never returned as a group. Sometime later, the investigation team informed the group that they would continue to investigate into the situation and assured all those of major concerned that the doors would be replaced at any cost. Six years has passed since they last received word of the replacements. As time passed the issue died. The Tenants learned to live with the situation.

The row homes section of Miller Homes seemed to be occupied by a group of people composing of different mentalities. The Tenants here tried to create a private-like setting for their area. Blankets of grass, although not nicely kept, managed to survive under light traffic of passer-bys. Occasionally, bushes of blooming flowers, fruit and vegetable plants would be seen growing close to the outlining structures.

Most of these Tenants showed signs of caring, but in reality they came to realize that no matter how hard they worked and how much help they received, Miller Homes would never be restored to its original beautiful creation. It grew to become known as a drug infested haven, coupled with low-income families and welfare recipients.

CHAPTER Two

The Story Begins

It was a late summer afternoon. The sun continued to cast a glowing blanket of heat across the earth's surface. Tenants running from abnormally heated apartments, gathered within the lightly shaded areas of the courtyard, produced by their towering high rise. The air was filled with a variety of adults and children voices and sounds while loud music from boom boxes made every attempt to override them. Several children danced and played throughout the area under the watchful eyes of their guardian. All seemed normal until a medium built, young black teenager, looking to have just turned fourteen came running at top speed from around Tower One's corner cutting a path across the earth's hardened covered surface, nearly plowed into several young girls playing Double Dutch who seemed to be in his traveling path. With the use of a few tricky, dancing steps, the young boy managed to dodge pass the girls as he quickly made his way toward the towering building. The back of his tee shirt could clearly be red saying, *Hands Off*, as he started to fade from the partly sun lighted area and into the building.

Second later, two uniformed Police Officers came charging around the same corner, pressing their pistol into its holster with one hand and the other swinging wildly. They too, dodged passed the group of girls with a few dancing steps of their own. The girls immediately stopped jumping and quickly removed themselves from the area. The officers stopped directly in front of Tower One's doorway. Their eyes scanned the surrounding area. Not able to see the teenager they were chasing, came to a quick conclusion that the runner must have ducked inside the confronted doorway.

Not wanting to waste more time, the Black Officer led the way as the two rushed into the building only to find themselves in the midst of a lobby surrounded by empty floor space, a doorway with steps leading upward, an open elevator and several quiet people standing off to one side. Over the years, Tenants had grown to become leery of the police patrolling in and around Miller Homes due to their association with the drug dealers. They had resorted to becoming non informative regardless of how trivial or important the matter at hand might seem to law officials. The police, in return, over the years had grown to ignore relaying upon receiving assistance from these people. They took it upon themselves to rely upon their own individual judgment by taking matter at hand and dealing with the situations to the best of their knowledge and ability.

"I'll take the steps," shouted the tall thin Black Officer with a fast breathing pattern and speedy words. "You take the elevator to the fifth floor and go to the stairway. Watch to see if you see him coming toward you. Hold him until I get there. If he gets off the steps before coming to you, come down to where he turned off. Got it?"

The other Officer, a Caucasian, drastically over weight, nodded his head in agreement. He had become completely exhausted after participating in the chase. Now gasping for air and holding his sides, he tried to bend to his waist. But could not.

"Okay, let's do it," the Black Officer commanded. The Black Officer started to quickly move toward the steps, rounding the open doorway and disappeared into his climb. The sound of someone running above him echoed through the entire winding stairwell.

The other Officer managed to make his way into the elevator. Quickly he located the control panel and began pressing a dark fifth floor button. A few seconds passed. The door refused to move. He pressed it several more times. Still he waited and still nothing happened.

Finally, after becoming impatient, he began to swiftly beat against the button causing noise to spill out beyond the elevator's entrance.

A slow walking elderly woman, supporting herself with the aide of an African style carved walking cane, entered the building. Upon hearing the sound of pounding noise, she directed her steps toward the elevator to see what was creating such a sound. Upon entering the elevator, she saw standing along the front left corner, the officer continuing to hammer away as if he was driving something into the wall.

She became annoyed while momentarily watching him pounding away uncontrollably. "That's why these elevators don't work half the time," she spoke harshly. "It's nuts like you who don't live around here who keep these things broken down. Don't you see it AIN'T working?" The Officer pretended not to hear her as he continued to pound even harder on the panel button. She raised her cane as though to hit him but had second thoughts and held it in a pose. "Go around to your own neighborhood if you want to tear something up," she said angrily. Still he refused to acknowledge her. She could no longer control her angered and with a swift swing, hit him once with the cane across his back. In a rough tone of voice, she called out, "Of all the nerve! A grown man at that. You're worse than the kids."

He stopped, turned to look back at her. It appeared the Officer was in a state of frustration. He returned to hammering harder on the panel. "Lady, I'm in a hurry. This is a police matter."

She became wild eyed, and her lips begin to tremble. "So is that an excuse for doing what you're doing right now?"

Realizing he had just suffered defeat with the elevator door not cooperating, he gave his fist a good look before stepping from the elevator. A feeling of shame clouded over him as if to confess for his misbehavior.

After shortly entering the stairway, the Officer running up the steps no longer heard footsteps moving above him. He was too far below to guess which floor the sound had disappeared from. Upon reaching the fifth floor landing, he stopped to gasp for breath in his out of shape condition. Most of his energy had been consumed by the time he reached the fifth level floor. His partner was nowhere to be seen. He knew the elevator was able to out run the teenager even at the speed he was traveling, if he continued to climb the steps high enough. Something must have gone wrong below which was always a major problem. He walked to the elevator door. Placed his ear against it. No sound was heard inside. Discussed with the outcome, he backed off to give it a swift kick and stared at it momentarily. All he could do now was to turn around and head back down the steps. Minutes later, he did just that.

When he arrived in the lobby, his partner was standing inside waiting for his returned. The Black Officer looked at the elevator with its doors spread wide open. The White Officer hunched his shoulders as if to say, *'he got away, what's next.'*

Breeze's stroke of luck was running good this day. He had made it to the third floor, leaving the two Officers puzzled. He knew he had speed and a good knowledge of his way around the area. After all, this was his turf. He was born in this part of the City and lived around Miller Homes since he was younger in age. It had never occurred to him that there existed the possibility of him ever getting trapped off by the police. He knew he could duck in and out of several homes and apartments in this neighborhood because of his friendly relationship with the people. They had always thought of him as a nice quiet kid who was well mannered. Most of the adults knew him well. Most people couldn't picture him as being a member of a drug infested gang. He was the type of young person who didn't exploit his street knowledge in their presence.

Last Friday was his fourteenth birthday. This would make his fourth year in the drug business. He liked being a dealer. It set off a new way of life for him as an independent person.

When the two Officers spotted him making a deal in the parking lot, he ran off immediately, leaving the drugs with the customer and the latter fishing in his pocket for the going price. The customer was one of his regulars. This wasn't the first time Breeze ran off on a customer. He knew the customer would know how to handle that situation and return to pay him when the Officers weren't around. After all, he was in the best position to make the best deals. That's why the customers were always looking for him. But for now, he was making his getaway from a deal that had gone bad. He stood in the hallway for several minutes waiting for the officers to leave. Finally, after thinking the coast was clear, he made his way up to the seventh floor.

He walked swiftly down the hallway counting dollars he had retrieved from his hip pocket. The light coming from an open window at the end of a hallway served as his guide toward his chosen destination. A low sound of music began to fill the air as he continued to walk forward. He was going to Sonny Bee's apartment for refuge, just as he had done in the past.

Periodically looking up at the door numbers, he finally stopped at Apartment 721, taking a moment to stick the money back into his pocket. He looked in both directions. Not seeing anyone in the hallway, he began to slap on the door.

This was Sonny Bee's apartment. Breeze could tell, even without seeing the number, by the sound of music blasting through the door. Loud music was Sonny Bee's way of letting the world know he was alive. Breeze waited a few seconds, then hit the door with his fist and adding a few kicks in hope of increasing his noise over the music. Without any warning, the door opened. A tall, brown-skinned young man of nineteen years in age stood looking down at Breeze. Anger filled Sonny Bee's eyes as he squints them toward Breeze. "Are you crazy?" Blasting his voice in Breeze's direction. Breeze didn't say a word. "What's your problem? Didn't your Momma ever teach you how to knock on people's doors? Get your butt in here! Are you trying to break my door down or something?"

Breeze walked in. "No. Not really," his said calmly. He was use to Sonny Bee talking this way. Breeze ignored him. He liked the apartment. It had album covers featuring recording artist covering the walls of the front and dining room areas.

"Have a sit down somewhere, but not next to Sandy. The dog might want a piece of you."

"Solid." Breeze said as he found a seat on the opposite side of the room away from the girl and the dog. He seated himself and sat quietly looking at Sandy and the dog. Thoughts raced through his mind that there was something strange about the two of them.

Every time he asked questions concerning her and the dog, he never received a straight answer. Maybe it was none of his business, but he did know that every time someone came into this apartment and moved close to Sandy, the dog would let out a nasty growl.

Each time Breeze saw Sandy, she looked a mess. Her hair always needed combing. Clothes were filled with wrinkles and partly falling from her slender body. She always gave him the impression she was smiling at him. He tried returning the smile, but most of the time he came to the conclusion her mind was somewhere else in space. He returned his attention to scanting the room.

Sonny Bee had gone to his room to change clothes. He didn't stay long and now was returning. Breeze had always admired him since the age of ten. Sonny Bee was like a kingpin to him. This added up to good times and plenty of money. Sonny Bee was the biggest drug dealer in Miller Homes. Breeze saw Sonny Bee's prestige through being the only person in the area driving a new candy-apple red Jaguar with white interior and plenty of money. This was real big time merchandise in Breeze's eyes. This made him more eager to be closer to Sonny Bee.

Suddenly, there was a hard knock on the door that filtered through the sound of music. Sonny Bee went to see who was there. When the door opened, Scrap rushed in. He was a light-skinned, lanky teenager with a thin mustache and a little peach fuzz under his chin. He came in just far enough so Sonny Bee could close the door. Scrap stood motionless. Rage began to brew in his eyes. He looked around the room and spotted Breeze. With thunder in his voice, he shouted toward Breeze, "What the heck you trying to do? Get the whole posse busted?"

The whole room seemed to process a stillness like never felt before. Sandy got up to turn down the music. After doing so, she returned to her seat. Breeze continued to sit in cool composure, not saying a word. Sonny Bee froze where he stood just to listen. Scrap jerked his head in Sonny Bee's direction. "Do you know what this little punk just did?" Before Sonny Bee could say a word, Scrap blurred on. "Let me run it down to you. With all the Blue Knights in the world moving around down there, he got the nerve to be out there dealing."

Sonny Bee became surprisingly shocked "No, is that so Breeze?" He asked.

Breeze remained silent.

Scrap returned his anger toward Breeze. "Next time that happens, I'm gonna take all your stash, bust you myself until you learn to appreciate the value of this business." Scrap's eyes grew wild looking. "Yeah." In a cunning voice he whispered, "I'll take all your money. All your drugs. All your…"

"Later for you," Breeze interrupted in a shout.

"Ok, cool it," Sonny Bee interrupted. "You made your point. I'm not moved by all this. Let's go check out the turf and posse. I want to see what's up with all these so-called Knights invading our area. Sandy, I left a little something in my bedroom for you. You stay here. If anybody's looking for me, tell them I'm out of town for the day. You got that?"

She shook her head in agreement and turned to look out the window. Scrap continued to stare at Breeze. Breeze continued to be unaffected by his words and walked out, disappearing into the hallway. Next Sonny Bee, then Scrap followed.

The three walked in single file through the hallway, and started down the flights of steps.

About halfway down, Scrap grabbed his nose. "This place really smells bad." No one said a word.

Upon reaching the first floor, they headed straight for the courtyard.

"Go round up the posse and have them come to me," Sonny Bee instructed them.

Minutes later, a small group assembled before him. He looked them over roughly trying to detect whether or not they were spaced out on drugs. If they were, he would have to take a stand knowing it would be tough relaying his message. After a minute had passed, he spoke. "What's up with all these Blue Knights?"

Someone in the group voluntarily spoke out. "There was a fight in Tower Two. Somebody called the law and you should of seen'em coming. There were a thousand of them. Look like they were coming out of everywhere, cars, trees, you name it. I got paranoid and hid my stash. Now that they done split, things are back to cool again." Sonny Bee eyes shifted towards the parking lot.

"Okay, let's take care of business. The dollar gets the last word." Another member of the posse spoke up.

"We got problems."

Sonny Bee turned to face him. "Run it down to me. What you mean?"

"Flash and his posse been moving in on our turf. Some of his boys are on the way down here with a lot of high grade stuff to pass off."

A glow of anger appeared in Sonny Bee's eyes. "We gonna put a halt to this right now. Let's go show them who this tuff really belongs to." At that instant, he spotted Flash's posse coming into the parking lot. Sonny Bee led the way toward them. When they had advanced to within twenty feet of their rivals, Flash stepped out of a parked car and began walking toward his own posse. "I been hearing from my posse that your posse want to start a beef over this turf," Flash said harshly, looking Sonny Bee up and down. He continued walking until he stood directly in front of his posse, while holding his eyes glued on Sonny Bee.

Sonny Bee clenched his two fist together and cracked a few knuckles with both fist balled into one before placing his hands down and parting his feet. "Yeah," said Sonny Bee. "I'm going to be giving them more than just a beef." He pointed his finger in the direction of Flash's posse. "I don't give a damn what you dudes are thinking. If you got plans for the future, I suggest all of you split while I'm still in a mellow mood."

"Are you trying to tell me you planning on doing something to me and my posse?" Flash said, sarcastically.

"If you're smart, you'll figure it out."

Flash became stern. "This is America baby. Nobody owns any territories around here. We ain't moving out or away, now or ever. You better start learning how to share."

One of Sonny Bee's boys pulled out a handgun. He let it hang close to his leg while rubbing his trigger finger against the trigger. Flash took notice of this move during a few seconds of silence, but his expression didn't change. He feared no man, woman or beast. His posse continued to look on. "Let's go," said Flash. "It looks like war to me. Nobody tells us where we can't go to take care of business." He and his posse started walking away.

"This turf belongs to us," shouted Sonny Bee to the backs of the leaving posse. "We'll do whatever it takes to keep it ours."

Flash stopped for a moment, turned slowly toward Sonny Bee. He raised his arm with a killer's look on his face to point in Sonny Bee's direction. "You ain't seen the last of us by a long shot. We got weapons, too. And all the goods that goes with them." He turned and led his boys away.

Sonny Bee could hear Flash's posse mumbling in anger. "We ain't got to take that stuff off those punks. I'm gonna get mine."

Sonny Bee's group watched as Flash continued to walk his posse out of the Miller Homes parking lot and out of sight.

"That's the way to rap to them," Breeze said. "But knowing how crazy they are, they'll be back like he said. He means it too"

"I wouldn't loose any shut eye over them," said Sonny Bee.

CHAPTER
Three

Bertha was in her early thirties, unmarried and fair game for any young man who roamed Miller Homes. Her mannerism of walking produced a sway that could turn the head of a full glass of beer. She was such a marvelous attraction. Hair always cut short and well groomed. Skin having the smoothness of silk and eyes that would melt ice cubes. At times, her mannerism and appearance annoyed her greatly. She didn't enjoy being stared upon by people she didn't know, especially in this neighborhood where many of the males processed devious minds.

Living in Miller Homes had not been one of her favorite dreams. Since the first day she moved into her apartment, she knew she would be classified as a warehouse statistic where every day brought on new challenges. She couldn't call her situation living. It was more like a survival course. People packed in on one large block like canned sardines.

For the past nine years, this had been her home. However, the thought of moving away was always with her, but taking the first step seemed impossible. Money was the key factor in keeping her here. She hadn't worked in the past six years. The factory where she last worked relocated to the South, leaving her devastated. She tried finding other jobs, but her skills were limited to what she learned in the factory. In those days, there was very little opportunities available for retraining in skills that paid fairly decent wages. So in order to keep life going for herself and her two children, she resorted to enrolling in the welfare system. But after a couple years of being enrolled, the money seemed to grow smaller while her children grew larger. Rather than to abandon her two children, four years ago, she decided to give her two children away to different fathers whom she never married. One of them being a boy and the other a girl. The fathers became the parents of his child. But still being down on her luck, she was forced to remain here in Miller Homes.

Bertha sat by her fifth floor kitchen window in Tower One, overlooking the courtyard and most of the parking lot while soft music from a stereo set filled the apartment. She had been observing what was taking place below during the past hour with her girlfriend, who was also sitting at the kitchen table eating a sandwich and drinking from an ice-filled glass. "It's terrible the way these young kids are dealing drugs in this neighborhood," Bertha said in discuss.

"I agree with you one hundred percent," replied her girlfriend.

"We've been holding meetings downstairs with the Mayor's people. I sure hope they do something soon about them."

"Me, too," replied her girlfriend while reaching for her glass and preparing to take a sip.

"You can't even let your kids play outside without having to watch them. You don't know what's going to happen to them next."

Her girlfriend took a sip from the glass and placed it on the table. "I know what you mean. If I had kids, they'd probably never see daylight. I just ain't got time to stay out in that heat and watch'em."

Bertha laughed. "Ain't that the truth. And when I was out the other day, this young man, who I still call a boy, had the nerve to offer me some free crack if he could do something nice and nasty to me."

"That's awful."

"I tell you, it seems there's no respect for the female race."

"Women don't get the respect they deserve in the first place." Her girlfriend took a bite from her sandwich and laid the remains on a plate.

"You got to really be in a bad way to give up something for some drugs."

"Honey, a lot of them do and that's no lie," mumbling with her words.

Bertha looked her girlfriend straight into her eyes. "I admit I smoke a little weed every now and then. It ain't never hurt anyone that I know of, but them other drugs, girl, they will kill you two weeks back into yesterday."

"I know what you mean," her girlfriend was quick to reply.

"That girl living in Tower Two. What's her name?" She stopped to think.

Her girlfriend took a sip from her glass. "I know who you mean."

"They got her so hooked on that mess, half the time she don't know who she is or where she's at."

"We dealing with a whole new generation out there."

Bertha turned to look out the window for a split second. "Tell me about it."

"They ain't nothing like us when we were their age. My Momma use to be on me like bacon grease on grits."

Bertha went into an uncontrollable laugh.

"I have to smoke a little myself to keep my nerves straight."

"Me too," replied Bertha.

"I got a little something on me now. You wanna get fired up?" She reached for her pocketbook.

"No, not before I drop in on the Mayor's meeting this evening. I got some words for him that will make his toenails curl."

Her girlfriend started to laugh.

"Maybe later on tonight," said Bertha. "Right now, I got things to do."

"I got things to do, too. I'm sitting here like the world's gonna take care of my business. Let me get myself out of here. It's getting late." She ate the last of her sandwich, then opened her pocketbook, fumbled around inside before taking out a little brown envelope and a pack of rolling papers. Bertha watched as she rolled a joint and laid it on the table. "This is for later if you want to get your grove on. Thanks for the sandwich."

"Don't mention it. If I got food, you welcome to it. That's what friends are for, to share what we think should be shared and thank you for the joint."

Her girlfriend put the contents back into her pocketbook, rose from the table and walked toward the door.

Bertha followed her into the hallway. "It's along walk to the first floor."

"I know. Maybe I should smoke one of these joints before I start going down."

"If that's as good as you say, you won't know when you hit bottom." They laughed about it together.

"You're right. I'd better just go. Take it easy."

"I'll take it anyway I can get it. See you later."

Her girlfriend walked away. Bertha closed her door and headed back to the table where the joint lay. She picked it up, kissed it with a smile and placed it in a cabinet along the side wall edge. She pushed a cereal box against it so as to block it from view. While she was closing the door, there were three knocks on the door. *It had to be Butch*, she thought. He was the only person who knocked that way. She walked to the door, being careful to look through the small peep hole to ensure it was him before opening it.

Butch showed a smile as she let him in. Butch was younger than her by seven years. On many occasions, he would come to Miller Homes from across town. Instead of hanging out with the fellows most of the time, whose main concern was selling drugs. He would visit her. The majority of the dealers didn't like him. And he didn't care much for the either, but he needed money and a place to hang out. So, he chose this location as a part time hustle.

Bertha met Butch at a party about three years ago. She found him to be a pleasant and caring person. These were things she liked about him. That evening, they partied together and when the night was through, she took him to her apartment. From that night on, they have been the closes thing to lovers.

Now as he stood in her apartment's front room, she looked into his eyes while moving closer to kiss his cheek. He in turn, kissed her on the lips. They embraced gently. He whispered something into her ear as the music continued to play softly. She smiled as if enjoying the combination and suddenly pushed him away.

"You make my whole world come alive," she said cheerfully.

"And I want to be your whole world, also."

They walked to the kitchen table and pulled out chairs. This is where most people sat when they visit. He seated himself first and clasped his hands upon the table before him. She did likewise while looking straight into his eyes. After all these years, she still held a warm fascination for him.

His facial expression became serious as he stared back into her eyes.

"Dig this baby," he said, showing signs of uncertainty. "You know we been tight for years. Ain't that right?"

"Right honey!" She reached out to touch his hand.

"You know when I put your stereo in hock the last time you had it back in four days. Ain't that right?"

Her expressions changed. "Yeah," she said as she withdrew her hand.

He started to show signs of being a little timid while watching her momentarily and trying to figure out the best way to get his point across. "Well, dig this. I got a real deal going and I need money right now. Like, as soon as possible."

"Let me guess. You want to pawn my stuff again?"

"Well, you know. I could have it back in your hands in three days."

Her face took on a serious composure as anger started to set in. Her voice became stern as she lashed out at him. "How do I know you're not lying to me? You know I don't like doing this. I didn't like it the last time and I don't like it now."

He leaned toward her in an effort to try to touch her hand, but she was quick to draw it back. A smile appeared from the corners of his mouth. "This is a sure thing, baby." The words came out soft and natural.

"May I ask, just what is it you plan on doing or buying with the money?" She placed a strong emphasis on, "This time?"

"Baby, don't say it like that. All I ask is that you have faith in me. Have I ever let you down?"

She was starting to breaking down. "No."

"What's it going to be? I need the bread like I said, as soon as possible."

Silence filled the room as she continued to stare into his eyes. Suddenly, she looked away. "Okay. Make this your last time."

His smile grew a little wider. "Most definitely," he said, eagerly. "I plan on making a killing. Pawning your stuff will be history after this time."

She softened her voice. "By the way, how much am I getting out of this?"

He looked at her point blank. "Let me make the money first."

"Alright."

He couldn't wait to get started. Together they disassembled the set. She produced the original boxes from a closet and placed them next to him. He packed the component set while she watched.

"I sure hope you ain't messing around with them drugs again," she said.

He stopped cold and looked seriously at her. "Do I look like I'm doing something with drugs?"

"Not now, you did yesterday."

"Baby, I told you yesterday I was feeling real ill. People on drugs and people sick have the same look most of the time. Think! Sometime you should check it out." He went back to packing.

She realized she had said the wrong thing. "I'm sorry. That was the wrong question to ask. I guess you're right, my bad."

Minutes later, he had everything packed in four boxes and ready to go. The elevator had been out of order for weeks and he was afraid to ask Bertha for her assistance. So, he alone would have to make two trips down and up the stairs. *Why did she have to live so far up*, was his thought. If he wanted the cash, he would have to make the trips.

Flash and his posse left Miller Homes about three hours ago. In the meantime, Sonny Bee had taken Breeze with him for a ride to his secret place where he kept his stash of crack and other drugs.

Breeze was one of his two most trustworthy people. The other being Sandy. In return for his loyalty, Sonny Bee would give him free drugs and a little cash. By now, they were returning to Miller Homes' parking lot. The red Jag pulled into the last parking space at the far end of the lot. Sonny Bee turned off the ignition. He reached under his seat, pulled out a small bag and handed it to Breeze. "Take these hundred caps, pass them to the posse. You give me a count later, let me know what amount you passed off to each member."

Breeze took the bag, stepped from the vehicle. He proceeded to follow orders, but after traveling only a few feet from the car, he stopped, turned around confused. Thinking something wasn't right, he walked back to the side where Sonny Bee was resting with his eyes closed. The window was down. A low flow of music filtered out through it. "How many do I get for myself?" He asked with concern.

"Take fifteen," said Sonny Bee without moving.

Breeze rushed off.

A few minutes later, Sonny Bee opened his eyes. He saw Breeze taking the posse inside one of the Towers. Everything seemed to be under control. Lazy-like, he stepped from the Jag, looked around and eased his body up to sit on the hood of his Jag. He took a deep breath, held it in momentarily before slowly releasing it. Everything he had dreamed of wanting was at his fingertips. He couldn't help but to praise America. "I love it here," he shouted. Slowly he slid from the hood and walked toward Tower One.

CHAPTER Four

It had become evening by the time Bertha arrived at the meeting. All the seats were taken. She chose to stand in the rear of the crowd near a wall. As she looked around the room, she notice many of the people here were elders from the community. They talked among themselves. A few people she knew waved to her from across the room. She casually waved back.

A white man, wearing a dark suit, walked into the room followed by the two Officers who normally patrolled this development. The three walked to the front of the crowd. The dark-suited gentleman stepped onto a small platform. The two Officers retreated to a wall directly behind him.

"Please take a seat," the man asked gently. Those who stood took their seat while the noise started settling down to a low roar. The gentleman waited patiently. Bertha was the one person he had many unpleasant encounters with in the pass. At times, she had opposed everything he was trying to propose.

"I'm glad to see all of you this evening. For those of you who don't know me, I'm your Mayor, Thomas Knots. I'm here to listen to your complaints, and if possible, to help bring about a solution for them. I would like to start off by answering your questions one at a time."

An elderly man in the back of the room came to his feet. "What the heck's going on here? You promised us you'd have those drug dealers out of here three months ago. I ain't seen nothing yet."

"I can understand you being impatient for action," said the Mayor. "Everything takes time. We are in the process of acting upon it."

Bertha walked to the center aisle. "That's what you say," as she started walking down a narrow aisle in the direction of the Mayor. He looked straight at her. She was turning this out to be her meeting. He would have to deal with her. "Young Lady. Do you have something to say?"

She was all fired up. "I sure do." The words came out in a blaze.

The Mayor appeared to be a little on edge, but nevertheless, he remained calm. "I'll certainly be glad to hear it."

She stopped in a space between the seated crowd and the Mayor's table to face the crowd. "He says they're acting upon it. Look at the facts. This drug thing has been going on for as long as I can remember living around here. In fact, I heard about the drug problems around here even before I moved in. The cops are here, off and on. When they are here, they do little or nothing about the ongoing activities. I see them spending lots of time talking with dealers which leads me to believe they're working together."

"Hold it right there," said the Mayor quickly and spontaneously. "Those are very strong words. This police force is trained to uphold the law. Sometimes they may have to use measures which are unfamiliar to you."

She looked at him. "Do you expect us to believe that?"

"As a matter of fact, we are bringing our 'Say No Task Force' into this development in the next coming weeks. We want to train adults and kids who are willing to learn how to report ongoing drug activities as they see them. Sure, we want to get rid of these activities much more than all of you, but we need your cooperation. Our task force is willing to clean up this area. Hopefully, drug free."

She shook her head in denial. "How can you teach any kid to say no to drugs when they're making hundreds of dollars a day. Do you think for one fraction of a minute they're willing to give up that kind of income for minimum wages? NO! Their probably living in they're life of glory and can't envision it ever coming to an end. Some of them have been selling drugs so long, they think of it as a job. And as long as people keep buying that mess from them, you can count on these same dealers being in business for a long time to come."

"Hold it," the Mayor shouted. He could see Bertha had the crowd in her corner. He felt he had to get a word in to balance out the conversation. "We're locking up more and more of these drug dealers everyday."

"Who are you trying to fool. Go down to your jails sometimes and take a look at the situation as it exists, but you probably won't. Let me clue you in. They are so over crowded, you can't squeeze another person in there." She held up one finger, shook it a couple of times and pulled it down. "Not one! You of all people should know. Most often, all of those people being taken downtown are given numbers and told when to return for court appearances. Just where do that leave the drug dealers?" She threw up her hands. "Back on the streets."

The crowd erupted in an instant outburst.

The Mayor raised his hand as high as he possibly could in an attempt to quiet them down. "You have to realize when they come back for their hearing, most of them are given time to do. We have been transferring some of those convicted to less populated jails across the state. Now, about the kids, we are setting up programs that will provide training and jobs to show kids you can make money without selling drugs. We are setting up a series of lectures pertaining to good jobs based on taught skills and abilities. We are working on a system that will provide incentives for undesirable jobs. We will also give a series of lectures on the advantages between long term employment versus long-term jail sentences and freedom versus strict rules. We know kids are out to make money, but we want to teach them how to make it legally."

"The program sounds good, but you ain't gonna get kids to just volunteer."

"We know this. That's why our plan carries a choice as well as a chance. Anyone convicted for the first time will be given a choice, training or a form of detention in jail time. Second time offenders will be given a maximum fine and a maximum sentence. This will be spelled out to them. I think these plans will work when the person fines out that we're talking about football numbers in the form of a sentence."

"What about the kids seven and eight years old selling drugs? Are you going to lock them up or put them to work?"

"Of course not, these programs apply to kids thirteen years and older. Any kids under thirteen years of age will be put on file and returned to their parents. If that kid gets picked up for a second time, the person responsible for him or her, the parents will be fined for every offense committed thereafter. And those fines could get pretty stiff."

The crowd let out a loud burst of disagreement. The Mayor raised his hands once again. "Please let me finish." The noise died and he lowered his hands. "The parents must be held responsible for their own children. They should know where their kids are and what they're involved in at that age."

She was quick to intervene. "That's not always possible. So you stop one kid. You got new kids standing in line waiting to take their place." She became pretty stern. "The supply of new kids are endless. Money comes fast and easy for those kids who choose to go in that direction. I suggest you go back to your office and get your staff to draw up another plan." She started walking up the aisle toward the exit.

"Young lady," he called out. "You're not a realist."

Hearing those words, she stopped in her tracks, turned to face him head-on. There was a strong feeling of anger about her. "And you're full of bull."

Most of the crowd stood. Some waved their hands while others clapped and shouted overwhelmingly.

She turned back around and continued walking. The crowd continued to cheer after her. She opened the door and walked out, leaving the door to automatically close by itself. As she walked down the hallway, she could still hear the cheers becoming a loud commotion of anger. A feeling of accomplishment seemed to fill her with joy.

CHAPTER Five

Sonny Bee lay asleep in his bed with a slight smile protruding from his face. He was apparently having a pleasant dream. The alarm clock on a nearby nightstand produced a loud sounding ring. Quickly he rose the upper portion of his body. Swinging half wildly across the top of his night stand, he managed to knock over a partly filled glass of liquid. The crashing of glass against the floor shocked him into fully opening his eyes. Still moving his hand, he managed to smack the clock a couple times before silencing it. Seconds later, he fell back onto the bed with a sigh of relief. Another glance at the clock told him it was twelve noon. *What a way to start the day*, he thought.

He began staring into the ceiling. A blank look griped his face. Thirty seconds passed in a timeless moment. He felt the urge to rub his curly black hair with both hands. While doing so, he remembered a joint he left laying in the ashtray on the nightstand in the midst of a pile of ashes. Its size resembled a mashed up butt. The ashtray sat in the middle of the spilt liquid. Carefully, he retrieved the joint and propped himself up on one elbow to get comfortable. He tried placing it between his lips with two fingers, but it was too small. This came from his finest stock. It would be a shame not to get one more hit from the likes of this butt. A roach holder would solve his problem. He used it to squeeze part of a corner, then lit it with a lighter he retrieved from the wet nightstand. He took a long drag. The joint was more powerful than anything he had ever smoked. He tried to hold the smoke in, but it began to ease out, causing him to franticly go into a heavy coughing spell. He continued coughing until his eyes filled with water. Tears ran down his cheeks. The sheet served as a means to wipe away the tracks of water. "This is some dynamite stuff," he said loudly. "The toughest stuff. WOW! You can't beat this kind of rush anywhere." He returned the lighter back onto the nightstand, not caring at this point about the wetness. A glowing ash broke away from the holder leaving a trail of smoke floating into the air. He took a deep sniff from its stream, which mostly consisted of air. By now he had nearly reached his peak with the thought of even this little piece was too good to waste.

There was a string of tapings on the door. The dog barked. He extinguished the small stream of smoke still coming from his joint by mashing it with the sheet. For a few seconds, there was no movement in the room. His eyes began to close. Suddenly, they jerked open. The thought of someone at the door reoccurred to him. He swung his feet to the floor, located his slippers from nearby and slipped them on and headed for the door.

The dog barked. "Chill out, be cool," he called out. "I'm on my way." He grabbed his robe and was putting it on while making his way to the door. He unfastened the latch. The door seemed to have an ease of nearly opening automatically at a finger's touch. Two white men in black suite and black hats stood facing him. These were the men who supplied him with whatever drugs he needed. Sonny Bee had received stuff from them on credit, and now they were here to collect.

"Oh no!" mumbled Sonny Bee, as his face lit up in surprising fear.

"Oh yes!" responded the Boss man.

Sonny Bee backed away from the door.

They walked in uninvited.

The dog followed Sonny Bee from the bedroom and was now starting to walk toward them.

Having a slight fear of dogs, the second man placed his hand near a hidden pistol he wore.

The first man stopped. "Get that dog out of here, if you want him. We got business to take care of."

Sonny Bee walked toward his bedroom and the dog stopped to watch. The two men stood motionless while

Sonny Bee called for his dog, who went wagging his tail as he went into the room. Slowly the door was pulled closed and immediately, Sonny Bee went back to where the men were. By this time, the two men were picking through some of his personal items around the room.

"Look guys!" He said, showing signs of nervousness. "You can't just go picking through my stuff." He stopped just short of the coffee table. Neither man paid him any attention. "You guys going nuts or something?" He became angered. "You break anything, you bought it."

They stopped touching things. The Boss eyed him and walked up to him, almost being toe to toe. He looked deep into Sonny Bee's eyes. "You messing up real bad. You're three weeks late. Where's our doe?"

"I ain't got it," he replied boldly.

"I figured that. Word got back to me that you been seen flashing cash and picking up strays in that jukebox car of yours."

"You got your peopled mixed up."

He pushed Sonny Bee so hard, he went flying over the coffee table, landing flat on his back on the sofa.

"What are you trying to do?" he blurred out. "Blow my buzz?"

"We're gonna blow more than that. I ain't playing. The games are over. You got forty-eight hours to produce the twenty grand or picture yourself as dead meat. You go that?" He gave Sonny Bee one of those tough guy stares. Sonny Bee didn't say a word. "We'll be back. Don't try clearing out. If you do." The other man displayed his weapon non-emotionally.

"You don't scare me," Sonny Bee shot back defiantly.

"Just don't for your sake." They walked out, leaving the door open.

Sonny Bee continued to semi-lay on the sofa. Sandy came strolling into the apartment. "Do you always leave the door wide open?"

"Go away."

She was in a joyous mood as she went back to close the door. Her stingy voice seemed to crackle with a high pitched tune as she sang. "Beam me up Scotty, you control my body. All I want from you is for you to just be true, to meee."

"What do you want from around here?" he asked, in a harsh voice.

Her response was soft and sexy. "I want you and whatever you got to give."

"I got enough problems without you adding to them. Yeah, maybe I shouldn't treat you so good." He lifted himself from the sofa, filled with rage, and started walking toward his bedroom. She began to follow him. He could feel her catching up to him. He stopped suddenly, only to have her almost run into him. "Will you get off my back? I need room to breathe. I've been pushed around and followed enough for one day."

"Sonny Bee, I'll do anything." She looked sympathetic. "Anything for you. You treat me better than any man I know."

He went into his room. As he did so, the dog came out and when to sit under the window. Sonny Bee managed to shut the door in her face. The dog laid his head to rest across his left paw. Sonny Bee continued to fume with anger. He mumbled to himself while dressing. After slipping on his shoes, he removed his robe, rolled it into a semi ball and fast-balled it into an open closet.

Sandy was gone by the time he returned to the front room. The atmosphere was quiet. He walked out of the apartment, locking the door. For a moment, he stood motionless. "What a bad day this is gonna be." He began to walk away.

There was a study line of cars moving through the parking lot. Sonny Bee's posse was running from car to car passing out miniature bags with one hand and collecting cash with the other. Sonny Bee decided in a quick decision to leave them taking care of business. He would take care of some of his own.

He climbed into his Jag. Through his driver's side mirror, he caught a glimpse of Butch looking down at his watch, sitting on a car's hood in the middle of the drug action. This was the worse place to be if you weren't dealing. Anything could go down at any moment. "The boy has lost it," Sonny Bee said in a low voice. "If he had any brains, he'd be dangerous." He fumbled around in his glove compartment for a few seconds, then drove off.

Flash and members of his posse appeared on the scene just as Sonny Bee rolled away. Neither rival saw each other. Flash had come prepared to take care of business. "This is what we gonna do," he told his posse. He talked to them while eye balling Sonny Bee's posse scattered in the parking lot.

There were six of them that Flash could count off hand. When he had finished talking, they started walking towards the dealers. A few of Sonny Bee's members watched them making their approach. Others thought nothing of their presence, being they were hustling. Suddenly, Flash ordered his men to attack by saying, "Get'em." His men began to spread out in an assault manner. Sonny Bee's posse didn't know what was going on. They tried desperately to depend themselves. The battle was on. Both sides were engaged in heavy fist fighting. Sonny Bee's posse appeared to be losing.

Butch was unmoved by the action. He continued to sit calmly on the hood. Suddenly, someone jumped onto the hood attacking him from behind. He made various attempts to get away, but was thrown to the ground and beaten by two of Flash's members.

Sonny Bee's posse started falling to the ground. Flash's men went through their pockets, taking everything possible that could be taken.

Tenants, who had been sitting around the area, were used to seeing this type of so-called rough horseplay. Some looked on while others turned their backs to what was happening in the parking lot. Nobody called for the police. Nobody bothered to try breaking it up.

After Flash's posse had robbed all those who hadn't gotten away, they ran off like a pack of wolves.

They ran for some time at top speed until finally turning into an alley. Most of them were nearly out of breath. They stopped just inside an alleyway. Some of the members leaned against buildings. Others bent over, grabbing their knees. Half of them, including Flash, started coughing and spitting. Flash spotted a small box lying near one of the buildings. He walked to pick it up. It was filled with clean papers. He dumped everything to the ground and carried the box back to where his men were holding up. By this time, he was back to normal, but he could see his men were out of shape. "If you guys had to go on a run, I'd feel sorry for you. You couldn't make it. Put everything you got in this box. Let's see what we got."

Flash passed the box around. One by one each member emptied his pockets into the box. When the box was returned to him, he emptied the contents on the ground. There were dollar bills and packets of various drugs. He picked through them, collecting cash first while pushing the drugs off to one side. His eyes widened. A big smile appeared on his face. The posse had become delighted as well.

"Looks like we made a good score."

"Yeah," said one of the members. "Looks like we hit the mother vein."

"Yeah, if we can't get in on the action, we'll let them do the hustling and we'll do the collecting. They can have that territory."

Every member agreed as they chuckled. By now, they were breathing normal. Flash counted the money. Then began passing out small quantities, not forgetting to count himself twice. When he had given himself the last dollar, he reached down and picked up several packets of drugs. "You guys sell these and bring the cash to me."

"Do you think we're some kind of chumps?" asked Curly.

"Of course not," Flash answered, giving him a smile. "This is an organized posse." His face changed to seriousness. "You give me the money after you sell the drugs, I'll pass it out." He pointed to himself. "You got that? I'm king around here." No one said a word. Flash walked away.

Bertha walked out of the high-rise into a blistering heat of sunlight. She shaded her eyes by placing one hand against her eyebrows. On a nearby bench, she spotted Butch holding his head down. Something looked wrong. She could see a red substance smeared along side of his face. This gave her cause to be alarmed as she wasted no time in running to sit by his side. His eyes were closed and not aware of her presence until she touched the blood filled section. He jerked around instantly. She pulled her hand back quickly with horror in her eyes.

Blood trickled from his nose, down across his bruised lips to form little circles on the concrete.

"What happened?" She asked on the verge of crying.

"I got robbed," his mumbling voice was low.

She became confused. "What, how, who robbed you?"

"Flash's posse took me by surprise. They took the cash I got for the stereo set." He became angry. "Damn! I was waiting for this dude so we could make this deal when it happened. They attacked me without warning."

"Oh baby, what am I gonna do now?"

He lifted his head, looked her straight in the eyes. "Don't worry," he replied in a strong voice. "I'll get it all back even if I have to kill them suckers."

She started crying. "I knew I shouldn't have given you my stereo set."

He placed his arm around her back to console her. "You did the right thing."

"No, it's too late." She couldn't take her eyes away from his injuries. "Let me get you some medical help."

She started to stand up. "No!" He managed to say abruptly, grabbing her arm. "It's not that bad. Losing the cash hurt worse then what happened to me."

"Then let me get you to my apartment so I can help remove some of that blood from your face. You look a mess."

"I don't know if I can make that hike."

She tried to encourage him. "You're tough," she said. "With a little help from me, you can make it."

He started to ease from the bench. She placed her arm around his waist to keep him sturdy. They stood momentarily, then started moving toward the Tower.

He smiled at the thought of her helping him. "Ain't this a shame, you helping me," he said in a way of setting her at ease.

She smiled, "Everybody needs help sooner or later. And you're no exception."

They reached the stairway. He looked up to see how far they had to go. His look shifted to her. She stared back at him.

"Ain't no way," he said.

"I know you can," she replied. "Say it."

He shook his head in a negative manner.

She repeated for the last time. "Say it."

He shook his head again, but not as hard. "My throat hurts."

"You're talking now." She folded her arms across her breast, tightened her lips.

He could see they weren't getting anywhere with their stubborn attitudes. "Okay! I know I can."

She seemed to instantly come back to life and placed her arm around his waist. He sucked in a little air to artificially give him strength. Together they started upwards. But after traveling up one flight of stairs, he became weak from the pain eating away his body. His weight was such that she could not support him which caused him to slide into a sitting position. She, herself, feeling tired sat beside him.

As he sat resting, he looked around the small area until his eyes came to rest upon a hand painted number 2 over the hallway entrance. Reoccurring thoughts began to trouble him. "I can't believe Flash would let them pull this kind of stunt on me," he said.

"You should know he was never your friend. The only people who seem to like him is his gang. And that's probably because half of them are afraid of him. I think he's crazy."

"I guess you're right." He sucked in a deep breath of urine laced air. The odor made him start to cough. "Somebody ought to hose this place down," he said weakly.

"If you'd start moving, it probably won't smell so bad."

He thought about it for a few seconds. "Okay, I'm ready. Let's try it again."

"Three more to go," she said in a gentle tone of voice as she helped him to his feet.

They continued upward until finally reaching the fifth floor. By now his pain had grown worse. He held onto her going down the hallway until reaching her door. He leaned against the wall near her entrance. She took out her key to unlock the door, and wasting no time, helped him inside. They went straight to the bathroom where he started cleaning his face over the sink. Suddenly he stopped wiping, looked into the mirror. "The more I think about it," he said, "the madder I get. Do you know where I can get my hands on a gun."

"Hey," she said seriously. "I'm not gonna to be no party to no murder."

"This ain't murder. This is called pay back. Can you dig it?"

"No," she said point blank.

Sonny Bee pulled into the parking lot and immediately located a parking space. Breeze ran to him bursting with excited. Sonny Bee let his window down.

"Flash's boys ripped us off," he said in a forceful manner. "But I managed to get away."

Sonny Bee looked shockingly at him. "What do you mean, they ripped you guys off?"

"They attacked the posse and took their money and drugs."

He couldn't hold back his emotions. "They What?"

"They took everything. Wiped us out."

"Round up the posse. Get them over to my apartment."

Breeze ran off. Sonny Bee got out of his car and stood for a few seconds near the opened door. Suddenly, he whirled around, banged his fist against the roof. "Damn if I'm gonna let'em get away with this. Pay back is gonna be hell." He slammed the door, and proceeded toward his building. Someone left an empty can standing in the middle of the walkway. With intensity, he kicked it away from his path, causing it to skyrocket off into a barren, dirt filled area.

Downtown at the police station, two policemen from Miller Homes were standing tall in front of the District Police Chief's desk. He was very disturbed as he leaned back in his cushioned armchair.

"You two bone heads," he stared at them, "together are worthless. During your assignment around Miller Homes, neither one of you have yet to make one arrest in the last year." The intensity of anger was starting to brew within him. "Both of you are a total disgrace to this Department. I might be better off putting my ten-year-old grandson down there on patrol." Neither men spoke. The Chief looked at one than at the other.

"Tell me one thing either of you accomplished since being over there?"

The White Officer inched the brim of his hat around in front of him. He looked the Chief straight on with a smile of confidence. "The Tenants tell us our presence has slowed down the drug trafficking."

The Chief brought his chair forward to its normal position. He slammed the palms of his hands on top of the desk. "I don't want it slow down." He raised one fist to bring it crashing on the desk with a loud thump. Both officers jumped. The officer stopped moving his hat.

"I want it stopped!" His voice was loud and directive. "Do you hear me?"

Both officers looked at each other and turned to face the Chief. "Yes Sir." Their answers flow out together.

"This is the last time I want to see either of you in this office about this matter. The next time your badges will be in here without you. Do the both of you understand?"

They began showing signs of nervousness. "Yes Sir," they replied.

"Now get back to Miller Homes and let me see what you can do."

They turned and started walking toward the door. "And while you two are over there drifting around," the officers stopped to face him, "see what you can find out about a reported gang fight that happened yesterday. Do you think that's too, difficult?"

"No Chief," said the Black Officer.

The Chief looked to the other officer. "And you?"

"No Chief," he replied hastily.

They continued to stand motionless. The Chief waved his hand as if to ward off an incoming insect. "Okay, go. Just get down there."

In leaving, they walked through an office area of personnel seated at their desks. Most of the office people knew the two officers as the odd couple. They were always subjected to remarks pointed towards them. "How's the fat and skinny patrol progressing?" said a plain clothed officer. Another immediately joined in. "There goes the bopsy twins." "Give my love to the Miller Homes Children," came from another.

The two officers didn't respond. Their faces remained expressionless as they continued walking through the doorway. Outside, they found their patrol car nearby and drove away. The Black Officer was the first to speak. "That black kid, you know the one we chased into the building that got away?"

The other officer had to think for a moment. "Yeah! What about him? I see him a lot with that tall kid who drives the red Jag. That sure is a nice car to be had by a kid like him."

"I think we should start by talking with the kid who was on the stairway."

The White Officer looked surprised. "How the heck are we gonna catch him?"

"Easy," said the Black Officer. "Just simmer down. If you've been noticing, when he doesn't have any drugs on him, he won't run from us. That's when you can walk up to him."

"Come to think of it, you're right. There was times when he's even walked up to me."

"Listen, when we get over there, we'll have to ask around. Somebody might give us some information on him."

The White Officer seemed confused. "What's so special about him?"

"He's young and I can probably con him into talking."

They pulled into a parking spot around Miller Homes' and exited the car. The hardware had shifted on their bodies to an uncomfortable position. They took time to adjust everything back to where it was supposed to be. The Black Officer took the lead as they started walking toward the mass of people centered in the courtyard. Breeze was nowhere to be seen. They began by questioning kids around the area. All gave negative responses. Finally, a group was willing to cooperate. One kid looking to be at least eight years old, thinking he knew everything, was eager to talk. "He goes in there all the time," pointing to Tower One.

"When is he usually here?" asked the Black Officer.

"He comes around lunch time, but mostly in the evenings."

"Tell me where he hangs out when he's here?"

All the kids started looking around but only the same kid continued to speak. "In the parking lot and over there in front of that building." He pointed to Tower One again.

The White Officer scratched the back of his head. "That's the same high rise we chased him into."

"You want something with him?" asked the same kid.

"Nothing important," answered the Black Officer.

"Oh! I thought it might have something to do with the fight."

Both officers became surprised.

The White Officer knelt down on one knee to look the kid straight in the eye. "Do you know anything about the fight?"

"No, I just saw them fighting and Breeze running away."

"And what else?"

"That's all. My Momma don't want me near the parking lot."

"Thanks", said the Black Officer. "You have a smart Momma." They started walking their patrol area to discuss things between themselves. "We'll hang around here to see if he shows before our shift ends."

"Good idea."

Bertha passed a joint to her girlfriend as they sat at the kitchen table.

"This is pretty good stuff," said her girlfriend, holding it up with two fingers. Bertha let out a stream of smoke she had been holding in her lungs. She placed her hand over her chest as if to cough but didn't. "It sure is. Can you get me some of this?"

"You bet your sweet buns I can."

The way she said it made Bertha laugh. Her girlfriend joined in.

"Get me a nickel," said Bertha.

"No, lets get an ounce. We can spit it. No telling when I might run into something this good again."

Bertha was all perked up. "Okay, sure enough. I should be able to get some money from my son the next time he drops in."

She placed the joint in an ashtray that had been resting near the center of the table.

"That's a fine son you have. How old is he now?"

"He just became a teenager a few years back, smart, too." Her thoughts of him became evident. "I hope when he grows up, he'll find a nice young lady who will treat him right."

"I see him often in my travels. He looks a little big for his age. I wouldn't be surprised if those older girls aren't chasing him now."

Bertha smiled. "They better not. I would hate to see him with one of those Hoochie Momma's."

They smiled to each other. Her girlfriend took notice of a bare space next to the sofa. "Something's missing. Where's your stereo set? I thought it was awfully quiet in here for some reason. You usually have it on and turned down real low."

"Child, I don't want to even talk about it. It's a long story and I can't even begin to explain it."

"It must be bad if you can't talk about it."

Bertha perked herself up and extended her arms toward the table's center. "So when can I expect to get my part of the smoke?"

"When I get it," her girlfriend's tone of voice was sassy. "You can pay me after you test it." She looked at her watch. "It's getting late. I got'ta be going. I got a bunch of things to do."

Bertha smiled. She was feeling good. "You're always tied up in some action."

"I try to. There ain't no shame in my game." She placed the little bag and rolling papers inside her pocketbook, tucking it under her arm as she rose from her seat and started walking toward the door.

Bertha followed her, being careful to watch her starting to drift to one side. Bertha was quick to reached out and grab her arm. "Girl, you better slow down."

"I told you this was some good stuff. I feel like I could just fly out of here." She raised her arms. Bertha let go. "I'm a bird," she called out.

Bertha broke out into a burst of uncontrollable laughter.

Her girlfriend started flapping her arms as if to take flight.

"You're just too much for me," Bertha said. "Just don't try flying to the bottom floor from here. It's a long fall with many stops along the way."

"Tell me about it," she said as a smile stretched across her face. They reached the front door. Bertha opened it. Her girlfriend walked out still flapping and headed down the hallway. Bertha watched until she disappeared through the exit.

The meeting had just ended in Sonny Bee's apartment and everyone was filing out. Sonny Bee made farewells jesters to each person as they passed before him. The last man to exit stopped directly in front of Sonny Bee. Jesse was a long time close friend of Sonny Bee. When Sonny Bee started the gang five years ago, Jesse left his old gang on the other side of town just to be a member. He claimed Sonny Bee showed more loyalty to his men.

He stared straight into Sonny Bee's eyes with a feeling of depression. "I should have had my piece."

"I can dig it Jesse." He was quick to agree with Jesse. "We're gonna take care of them dudes."

Jesse gritted his teeth so hard, his teeth made impressions against his jaws. "I'm gonna get with them punks real soon."

Sonny Bee could see he was upset. "We can do this as a team."

Jesse ignored him. "I got what they need." He turned and walked out the door. Sonny Bee could see he was serious. Jesse couldn't stop babbling to himself as he walked down the hallway. "I got just what they need."

Sonny Bee closed and locked the door shaking his head in disbelief. Sandy had been sitting by the window all this time, stood and ran to put her arms around his neck.

"What the heck got into you," he asked.

"I love you so much," she said in a low sexy voice. "I hate to see you like this. I want to take some of that pressure from you, real bad." She sexually licked her lips.

He took her hands away and looked directly into her eyes. "You're a crack head. I don't mess with those types of women."

"I know you love me. I often see it in your eyes."

"If it wasn't for the fact that I trust you with my drugs, I wouldn't even have you around me."

"Don't change up on me. What can I do to make you love me?"

He threw up his hands. "Nothing!"

She gave him a little smile. "You just trying to be tuff."

"Don't you understand what nothing means?" He began to calm down. "Look, I ain't got time to explain it to you. Do me a favor, go back to your chair by the window. Let me know if you spot Flash or any of his posse. That's something you can do for me that I like. It's also a sign of loyalty."

She walked away toward the window in an evil mood. "That's all you want to do is use me for one thing or another. Someday I'm gonna find me a man who appreciates a good woman."

He couldn't hold back an out burst of laughter. "Good, do that. When you add up all the free crack I've given you, I don't think you don't know what those words mean." He went into his bedroom, shutting the door behind him.

Sandy sat near the kitchen window watching the kids playing below. She was angry, talking in a low voice. "That bum. He don't like women. He don't like men. Maybe he's queer for himself. I don't look that bad." She patted her hair as if to be putting it back into place, then stood up and went to look into a decorated wall mirror surrounded by album covers. She took a good stare at herself, moving her head from side to side. "In fact, I think I look better then some of those movie stars." She unbuttoned the top two buttons of her shirt to reveal a little more flesh. "Heck yeah," she said.

Sonny Bee walked around his bedroom thinking strong, when something came to him. He stopped at his nightstand, taking a small flat metal box from the bottom drawer. Inside was fifteen thousand in one hundred dollar bills. He stared down at the money while talking to himself. "I got until tomorrow to get five more grand. Maybe if I give them half when they return, I can hold 'em off for another week until the rest comes through." He thought about it. "Yeah, that's what I'll do." He put the money back into the draw and closed it.

He left the night stand and moved to the dresser where he picked up four little clear capsules containing some sort of white substance resembling rocks. After staring at them for a few seconds, he carried them to where Sandy was sitting by the window. "Did you see any of them yet?" he asked.

"Them who?" She asked, surprisingly.

"Flash's posse." He made a flurry motion with his hands. "What did I ask you to do? Can't you remember anything?"

"My memory is better than yours. No, I didn't see them yet."

"I told you. You're all cracked out. Maybe you're better off this way. Here's a few more." He dropped them into the palm of her hand one at a time. "One, two, three and four. Go for it." This was his way of paying her for doing good deeds.

She beamed with joy as if she had just received a fortune.

He looked at her while she stared into her palm and wondered how anyone could be this happy over drugs. For him, a little smoke every now and then was good, but it wasn't that good where it gave him cause to use it everyday.

The dog barked, breaking his chain of thought. That's when he remembered he had to tell her something. In a low voice, he spoke to her. "Don't forget to feed the dog."

She quickly closed her hand while jerking the drugs to her chest as if someone was grabbing for them and looked Sonny Bee straight in the face. Anger had replaced her smile. "It's always that stupid dog. Feed it. Take care of it. Walk it." Then she went silent.

He headed for the front door. She started mumbling in a soft voice. It was just barely audio, but he didn't have time at the moment to get into a hassle with her. When he reached the door, he looked back at her. She had gone silent with one elbow propped upon the table with the side of her face resting in its palm and looking off into another direction.

He opened the door and eased out into the hallway, making sure not to slam it shut.

She looked around realizing he had left. Even more furious now, she talked loud hoping he would hear it traveling through the air as he walked away.

CHAPTER Six

Butch managed to get his hands on a pistol. Now, he wanted to find Flash and get his money back. Flash was known for hanging around Miller Homes after dark. That would be the best place to find him. This is where a lot of weekend party goers would come for their drugs and Flash would do anything for money. He'd rip off a few party-goers and some Tenants if his timing was right.

It was dark when Butch arrived at Miller Homes. He would be brave this evening by taking Flash on, one on one. This way he could show the gang members he had heart. The area he selected was dark, away from overhead hanging light, but near the parking lot leading to the courtyard. This is where Flash would pass if he showed up this evening.

Flash was one of those bad guys who thought he couldn't be stopped. He led his people to believing he was immortal. This was the right time for Butch to strike to make Flash feel he could die like anyone else by putting two or three bullet holes in him. It might start him to thinking about dying and straighten his life up.

Butch took out the thirty-eight special he had bought. Not knowing anything about pistols, he asked the seller to load it and explain a couple of things he should know about the pistol. Butch was able to locate and press a side button which allowed the cylinder to roll out of place in the poorly lit area. Looking over the rear part of the pistol, he began to get scared. What if he pulled the trigger and nothing happened? "No," he said as he shook his head. Talking to himself, "No one would even think about selling a pistol that didn't work." He pushed the barrel back into place, raised it to aim at an imaginary figure. Slowly he lowered it and put it back into his pocket.

Two hours passed. The sound of voices could be heard coming toward him. At first he couldn't make them out, but as the voices grew nearer, he was able to identify one of them as Flash's voice in the crowd. When the voices grew within shooting distance, Butch stepped out far enough so his outline could be seen.

"Hello Flash. I see you're returning to the scene of the crime." The chattering stopped. The bodies kept coming forward.

"Who's there?" asked Flash.

"Stop or I'll shoot your head off."

Flash and his posse stopped. They stood motionless in the dark.

"I said, who's there? Is that you Butch?" Flash's voice didn't change. It was calm.

"Yeah," he answered in a scared voice. The posse started laughing.

"What you gonna shoot us with, your finger?" asked Flash.

Butch stepped out into the very small lighted area coming from one side of the building. He exposed the pistol so it was slightly visible to Flash and his posse.

"Oh, you got a gun," Flash said in a joking manner. "What we supposed to do, shake? All right boys, shake a little for the big guy with the gun."

"Hey man," Butch's voice grew intense, "this ain't no game."

"Talk to me. Don't you know you can hurt somebody with that thing? Put it down and let's talk. What's up with you anyway?"

"You damn skippy knowing what's up. I want the money your posse took from me when you guys jumped me."

"What if we ain't got it?"

"Then you'll get what this pistol has to offer in return. I'm here to kill if that's what the end results call for."

"You're a tough dude. I like your style. Did you get that way from watching television? One of those John Wayne flicks?" The posse started to laugh.

Butch's gun hand started to shake. His mouth quivered. Words poured out with a sign of fear. "Cut the B.S. Give me my money. I'm going to count to five. If you don't have it out by then, I ain't gonna stop shooting until this gun is empty. All these bullets are for you. If some of your posse want to share them with you, let them act stupid. I'm counting, one, two."

Flash reached inside his shirt.

Butch straightened his arm as he raised the pistol chest high.

Flash shifted his hand to his back pocket.

"Don't be acting stupid," said Butch.

Flash's voice became more serious. "I'm getting the money."

"Three."

Flash pulled out something.

Butch stared into the darkness trying to identify anything Flash might be holding, but couldn't.

Flash started moving in the direction of Butch. His posse stood motionless.

Butch stopped counting, anticipating to see signs of money. His hand continued to shake. He had lost most of his nerve to pull the trigger, but in spite of it all, he kept the pistol pointed. His urge to move in closer drew fear from fear of the posse's willingness to attack, pistol or no pistol.

Finally, Flash stopped, held something out in front of him. "Here it is," he called out. "Where do you want me to put it?"

"Lay it on the ground and back off."

"Anything you say, tough guy." Flash bent one knee to the ground.

Echoes of shots rang out.

Butch dropped his pistol. It produced a short flash of light as a single bullet rocketed into the dark of night. Seconds later, Butch fell to the ground on top of it.

Flash and his posse moved in closer to where Butch lay. Flash could see Butch moving his arms. When Flash was standing directly over Butch, he pointed his pistol straight down, firing one shot into Butch's head. He raised the pistol to his mouth and blew away the smoke coming from the mouth of the barrel.

Flash had the look of a savage on his face. His posse began to scatter in different directions. Flash recomposed himself, then, he too, ran off.

The next day, word had gotten around that Butch was killed by unknowns in a gun fight. The Mayor was informed about the killing before it reached the newspaper. Immediately, he had flyers printed, calling for all Miller Homes Tenants to attend a special meeting he was scheduling for tomorrow evening. It was the job of the two police officers to distribute this information. They set out on foot, carrying out this task.

"I hate to see anybody get killed around here," said the White Officer. "It had to happen sooner or later. I'm glad we were off duty."

"Yeah, that's for sure," said the Black Officer. "Chief would have for sure suspended us. I don't know about you, but I need my job." The White Officer stopped in his tracks. He looked surprised. "Oh, you don't think I need my job, too?"

The Black Officer stopped, turned around to face him. "Come on, I didn't mean it like that."

They continued on their way, each taking turns in eyeing the height of both Towers.

"If you expect to make it to the ninth floor passing out these flyers, you better start loosing weight." The Black Officer grabbed and squeezed the fatty part of the White Officer's body that was sticking out around his belt. "Looks like some healthy pistol grips to me."

The White Officer slapped the Black Officer's hand away. "Hey, watch that. You queer for my body?" There was a moment of silence. "Keep your hands off. This is prime choice." They laughed about it.

"Okay," said the Black Officer. "We'll start with me taking Tower One. You take Tower Two. Whoever gets back down first, wait for the other in front of your building. Most likely I'll get through first. If either one of us have problems, we'll communicate by walkie-talkie."

"Good idea."

"Talk to you later."

They split up. Each going his own way with one hand and arm filled with papers. The White Officer dropped a few sheets in front of his feet. He stopped to pick them up. Suddenly, he stepped over them and continued on his way.

On the fifth floor of Towers Number Two, Scrap and another member of Sonny Bee's posse were doing crack in a far corner of the hallway. These two were better known as users rather than sellers. Sonny Bee didn't care much about their habits. He needed them as part of a show of force to keep other gangs from taking over his territory.

The two dealers sat beneath a window with their backs against the wall. Sunlight coming through the window seemed to glide over their heads, touching pieces of liter spread out along the hallway floor. Both dealers continued to sit with their backs against the wall getting high and talking to pass the time of day.

"What's with that broad that hangs in Sonny Bee's apartment all the time?" asked Scrap's friend.

"I don't know, man. This might be little too deep for you to catch."

"Run it down to me anyway. My head is bad. I can catch anything."

Scrap rolled up a joint and handed to his friend. Friend took a long drag, held it in for a few seconds before passing it back. Scrap was quick to take a drag. He dropped his head. A trail of smoke came oozing from between his lips. The partially opened window above drew a thin line of smoke from them to vanish into the outside air.

"Some years back," said Scrap, "Sonny Bee use to use her to make money. She's a freak to the first degree. Yeah, guys use to pay Sonny Bee money just to come up to his apartment and watch her get laid by that dog."

Scrap's friend eyes grew wide. He changed his sitting position to sit in front of Scrap, but moved back because the sunlight was shining directly into his eyes. "That's wild," he said wildly.

Scrap kept his same composure. "She never knew he was making money out of the deal. Half the time, she was stoned out of her mind. That broad did a lot of crack during some of those years and a lot of tricks with that dog. Sonny Bee just out right gave it to her. Her and that dog still get down I hear. That's why she still hangs around over there and that dog pictures her as his thing. Was you thinking about taking her on?"

"You know, the longer I look at her, the better she starts to look. I told myself that a failure wasn't anything but a try and I ain't got anything to loose. I thought I'd give it a try. After hearing you run this down, I'd feel safer with Old Nelly Palm and her daughters."

Scrap broke into an uncontrollable burst of laughter. His friend joined in. Scrap had to wait until his friend calmed down before continuing to speak. "Sonny Bee told me she's been laying with that dog so long, she don't even want to be bothered with any dudes. Her life is centered around some crack and that dog."

"Yeah, that's wild. Have you ever seen that dog getting off on her?"

Just then, the White Officer came walking through the opened doorway. The two gang members were so high and engrossed in their conversation, they failed to take notice of the approaching officer. He stopped at the first door, bent down, pushed a sheet of paper beneath it and continued to move toward the two guys sitting.

Scrap passed a crack pipe to his partner. He took an extra long drag. It made him cough.

The officer looked in their direction when he heard the noise. By this time, the officer was only three doors away. When they happened to look up to see the officer staring at them, they tried to hide the pipe. But the officer viewed everything. "Hey, what you guys got there?"

"Nothing!" responded Scrap.

"Yes you do. Pull it back out." He gave them a couple of seconds. "Come on, let me see it." He placed the stack of papers on the floor without taking his eyes from them. *They might be dangerous*, he thought. He didn't know what to expect. As he moved in closer, he removed the strap from around his pistol and placed his hand on its handle. He stopped when he was about ten feet away. The two remained in the same spot barely moving their hands.

"Come on, I know you can move faster than that."

"I said I ain't got nothing. I checked myself."

"Me either," said his partner.

"Stand up." He watched them as they stumbled around getting to their feet. "Turn around, face the wall. You on the left, move over about six feet. Don't try anything. This gun has the power to blow a hole through you the size of a doorway. Both of you place your hands high on the wall and spread your legs." They followed instructions. He moved in closer to search Scrap first by running has hand around his waist, then quickly down and up one leg and onto the other. He stopped upon feeling something in one of the pockets. He backed off. "Okay, empty your pockets onto the floor with one hand. Keep the other high on the wall like you're reaching for J.C." First, the wallet came out. Scrap's partner turned his head to look.

"You on the other side. Keep your head and eyes straight ahead. You'll get your turn."

Scrap placed his hand back on the wall.

"Bring out the rest."

"That's all."

"No, there's something else in the front pocket. Let's get it out."

Scrap reached into the other pockets. Slowly he pulled out his hand balled into a fist.

"Drop it. Whatever it is, let it go."

The hand opened like a bomber dropping its load. Little clear capsules containing some type of crystallized substance crashed to the floor.

They spread out like roaches on the run.

"You're doing good, keep that hand working."

He reached into another pocket. This time he pulled out a folded stack of dollar bills.

"Okay, now you on the left, do the same thing." He did. The same results unfolded. The officer took out his walkie-talkie. "Tower One, this is Tower Two. Do you read me?"

The voice was a little broken up. "Tower Two, I hear you."

"Meet me down in front of Tower Two, I think we got something. Call for a wagon. We got a nice little pick up."

"Will do. Over and out."

The officer took out two sets of handcuffs. He threw each of them a pair. "Put them on tight." He waited until they had followed his orders, then moved closer to use a third set of cuffs to clamp those sets together. "Both of you move to one side," he said with trained eyes. He removed his hat, placed everything on the floor inside. He motioned for them to lead the way toward the stairway. The pair walked down the hall with all four hands tied together into a ball, resembling one unit. The officer was able to pluck the papers he had dropped from the floor as he started to follow them. The pair walked down the stairs almost tripping over each other until finally reaching the first floor.

They walked out of the building to see Tenants stop doing what they were doing to look onward. The Black Officer came out of his building around the same time the wagon arrived. He hurried across the courtyard to give his partner a hand. The driver immediately jumped out of the wagon, walked around to its back, pick through a ring of keys while facing the door. Upon locating the right key, he opened the doors, extending them wide. Scrap and his friend climbed inside with the help of both officers. They seated themselves near the door opposite each other. The driver closed and locked the doors. Then, returned to the driver's seat. Seconds later, the wagon sped away.

Breeze had been in the parking lot watching while they were being led into the police wagon. At one point, he stood close enough to touch them. After the wagon had disappeared from sight, he took off running up to Sonny Bee's apartment to inform him about the latest event. Banging on the door as usual, and gasping for breath, Sonny Bee opened the door surprised to see Breeze in a bending position and holding his knees. Breeze looked up to the see Sonny Bee with that same mean look on his face when he was going to chew Breeze out for going crazy on the door. This time Breeze beat him to the punch by starting up a quick conversation. "They got them," he said all in one breath.

"Slow down," Sonny Bee responded in a surprisingly, shocking tone of voice. "They got who?"

Breeze swallowed a couple of times, inhaled deeply then, let it out slowly. "Scrap and this other dude he hangs with."

"Who got them?"

"The Blue Knights took them away in the Knight's Chariot. You gon'na get them out?"

Sonny Bee's facial expression turned neutral. "Come on in. Don't just stand there."

Breeze walked in. Sonny Bee closed the door. Breeze faced him to see what he was going to say. Sonny Bee stood motionless for a moment. He stared into space. Slowly his head dropped. He looked into Breeze's eyes.

"No."

Breeze became immediately shocked.

"I ain't got nothing to do with that."

Breeze jerked his head straight up as his eyes popped open wider. "But they your boys, you know, posse members and all that stuff."

"Yeah, I know, but you got'ta remember, in this world, every man for himself. If you get caught, you got'ta keep your mouth shut and hope you don't get any time."

Breeze continued to be silent for the next few seconds. Suddenly, he spoke with a questionable look on his face. "Do you mean if the Blue Knights pick me up, you gonna let me rot in jail?"

Sonny Bee bent down on one knee in front of Breeze. He held him by the shoulder while looking into his eyes and remembering that he is just 14. "No. Not you. We're like brothers. It's the other dudes who would face the axe. They know what kind of chances they're taking. Look, you got to understand that this is a serious business. You can do good if you do the right thing. Or, you can screw up real bad. Nobody's backing up anybody in this business. Do you understand what I'm saying?"

Breeze looked a little confused. "I think so."

"Think about it sometime."

"So that day when Scrap was on me about dealing in the parking lot, is that what he was trying to run down to me?"

"Yeah, you're on the right track."

Breeze looked down at the floor. Sonny Bee got back on his feet. Breeze started looking around the apartment. "Where's the dog?"

"Sandy took him for a walk."

"It seems different when he's gone."

"I know what you mean."

"Well, I got to be going."

Sonny Bee opened the door. Breeze walked out. He stopped just as his second foot touched the hallway. "Here come those two white dudes dressed in black."

Sonny Bee opened the door wider, sticking his head out into the hallway to see for himself. "It's okay. You go ahead, I got things under control."

Breeze walked toward the steps, passing the two men.

Sonny Bee was still standing by the door when they approached his apartment.

"What do it look like?" asked the Boss.

Sonny Bee gave them a smile and a wave of the hand. "It looks great, come on in." All three went inside. Sonny Bee closed the door.

"Then you got the doe?" he asked with a serious voice and serious look.

"Do I look like I'd lie to you?" Sonny Bee held his empty hands out in front of him with both palms up.

"I don't want to see empty hands. Pass it over."

"I have to go into my bedroom to get it."

"We'll go with you just in case you're planning something." Both men made a motion to step forward.

"Just be cool," Sonny Bee replied. He held his arms up as if to be pushing them back. "No, are we taking care of business or are we taking care of business?"

The two men stopped. "All depends on what kind. I ain't into no monkey business if that's the direction we're taking."

Sonny Bee turned his palms up as if to offer something. "Trust me, I got the money."

The boss walked closer to stand toe to toe with him. "You ain't got it yet? I'm tired of waiting."

Sonny Bee went into his bedroom with a look of confidence. He counted out several hundred dollar bills from the envelope in his nightstand. He returned to the room where the men were. He handed the money over. The man counted it. Fanned it out. He looked up at Sonny Bee. The man looked angry. He slapped the money against his other hand. "What the heck is this mess, some monkey business."

Sonny Bee smiled. "No, dig this. I could only come up with half."

"Half?" he shouted.

Sonny Bee's facial expression changed from smiling to neutral instantly. "Will you let me speak?"

"Make it fast, this better be good. I would hate to see anything happen to you in the prime of your life."

"Okay, like I was going to say, that's half." He pointed to the money. His eyes followed his finger as he watched them start to shake. "That's all I could come up with." A scared look eased onto his face. "Come back next week and I'll give you the other half. Look man, I got it coming. That's real. I just can't put my hands on it at this minute."

"It don't work like that. You owe me. I want my money now. This ten grand." He shook the money in Sonny Bee's face. "I'm gonna keep this as interest."

Sonny Bee grabbed for the money, but the man was able to pull it back before he could touch it. "You can't do that." Sonny Bee balled his fist and made an ugly face. The other man pulled out his pistol, held it waist high. The Boss overlooked this action.

"You try grabbing this money again and I'll break your arm. I make the rules around here. You got until next Saturday. What I told you two days ago still goes."

Sonny Bee became calm again after see the pistol being pointed at him. "I'm almost out of product."

"That's your problem." He pointed a finger in Sonny Bee's direction. "Do what you have to. Think money or think consequences." He looked toward the man who came with him, nodded his head in a jester to go. Both men walked out. Sonny Bee stood in the middle of the floor burning with fury. He held both fist.

CHAPTER
Seven

Bertha was very upset about Butch's death. Over the years, he had become more than a lover. He was someone she could confide in. She shared her innermost secrets with him. He did the same with her. He shared his money, time, laughter and love. He was her breath of life. She was now forced to continue life without him. Most of her morning and half of the afternoon was spent getting high on the few small pieces of joints that lay within the apartment. She changed from her night clothes into a set of jeans, buttoned down shirt and white sneakers. She patted her small crop of curly hair in the absence of a mirror. She located her money nearby. Awkwardly, she managed to walk out of her apartment. She staggered down five flights of steps to the courtyard, talking to her self as if there was another person keeping up with her.

The courtyard was filled with children at this time of day. The sun was shining its ninety degrees plus temperature. She made her way to the parking lot with the intention of buying whatever she could to keep her high and to avoid these moments of great sorrow.

"Hey, Momma," one of the dealers called out in a soft silky voice. "I got something that will sturdy that walk."

She stopped.

He was a dark-skinned teenager around nineteen years in age. A member of Sonny Bee's posse who was a hard core drug dealer with an eye for any woman in her twenties.

"You talking to me?" she asked.

"Yeah baby, I'm talking to you."

"What you got that you think is so good."

He pulled a couple of small tubes from his pocket that resembled capsules. Feeling all spruced up, he strolled over to show her.

She stared down into his hand. They were so small she had to take a second look. "Those things look too small to do anything."

He was taken by surprise by the way she said it. He almost placed his hand directly into her face. "Say what? Baby, this is what's happening. One of these will knock your socks loose."

"I don't know about that. You got any marijuana?"

He ignored what she was saying with a smile as he looked her body down and up. "You know, I dig you.

Just to show you a token of our upcoming friendship, I'm gonna give you one of these for free." He held it out to her. She hesitated a few seconds before taking it. Wondering what to do with it next, she held it close to her face. "Okay, talk to me. What do I do with it now?"

He couldn't believe what he was hearing. He chose to go along with it. "I can see this is something new to you. Put it in the end of your cigarette."

"I ain't got none. I'm all out."

He reached into his back pocket, took out a half empty pack.

"Take one of these," he said as he stuck a finger into the package hole to make the opening wider. Flipping the pack sideways, he bumped the front end of the pack against the side of his hand. Several cigarettes appeared. He took one out and gave it to her. She just looked at it. "How do I get it in side. Is this some special kind of smoke?" she asked.

"Let me show you just how this thing is hooked up." He took the cigarette and the capsule. Showed her by doing it himself. He gave it back to her.

She placed it between her lips. He held out a match. She lit it by taking a deep drag. It started affecting her mind. "This is heavy," she said, shaking her head as if to wake up.

"I'll tell you what. You invite me to your apartment. I think you and I could really have a good time."

Her eyes grew wide. "I like this. You're on if you got more."

"Baby, I got a whole pocketful."

"Show me."

He reached into his pocket. She watched as his hand disappeared inside. It moved around gently, then stopped. She placed her right hand over the cleavage of her chest. She jerked her eyes up quickly to meet his. He gave her a pleasing smile. He pulled his hand from the pocket and extended a packet to her but it slid from the side of his hand. He tried to catch it in mid-air, but failed as it started to fall to the ground. Upon falling onto one knee, he was able to pluck it from the ground. She grabbed his arm as if to prevent him from getting away. He was pulled erect and was able to stand on his feet. Together they started walking across the courtyard toward her building.

After struggling to make it to her floor, they finally stood in front of her apartment door. She fumbled with her keys until finally locating the right one. She inserted it, and made a quick turn. The door gave a slight squeak as it swiveled inward. They stepped across an imaginary line. The two stood alone in a semi quiet spot of the front room. He returned his hand to his pocket. She looked deep into his eyes. The thought of Butch immediately returned to her. Her eyes began to water. "This guy I was going with," her voice was gentle and unbroken.

"Got himself killed all because he was hanging out in that stupid parking lot."

For a moment, he gave her a sympathetic look. "I'm sorry to hear about that." He held out his hand. "Maybe another one of these will help you forget."

"Maybe I do need to forget about him. He's gone and there's nothing I can do or say that will bring him back."

He took another capsule and pushed it into the end of a fresh cigarette. They smoked it together. When they had finished, he started feeling her body.

"That feels good," she said. He kissed her neck and lips. She responded by kissing him back. He unbuttoned her shirt. She unbuttoned his. He lifted her from the floor into his arms and carried her away toward the bedroom.

The sun shined directly on them through a crack between the side of the shade and the window frame. The light woke him up. He became face to face with a clock on a nearby night stand. Nine: Seventeen. He rolled over to face Bertha. Her eyes were still closed. He shook her lightly a couple of times and she squinted just before placing her hand up to block the light.

"Is this clock right?" he asked.

She responded with a delightful smile and agreed with a nod of her head. "It's been right every since I've had it."

He pulled the sheet from his body. Lifted himself into a sitting position, firmly placing his feet on the floor.

"Where you going?" she asked.

"I got business to take care of. Darn, I slept through the whole evening and night."

"We did sleep a long time."

He continued to sit on the edge of the bed.

She propped herself up on one elbow and covered her breast with her side of the sheet. "I liked that stuff you gave me. It made me become so alive. It was a lot better than those joints I was smoking. What did you say the name of that stuff was called?"

"Crack!"

She was surprised. "So that's what crack is like."

"Heavy stuff isn't it?"

"Yeah, I never thought I'd get involved with it. A lot of people say you can become addicted to it."

"It's what you make it. People become addicted to cigarettes, coffee and alcohol."

The surprised look disappeared from her face. "Yeah, I guess you're right."

He rose, located his clothing and began putting them on.

"Could I have a couple more of those?"

He stopped for a moment, looked down at her. She looked so sweet laying there that he couldn't say no. "I can't give you too many. I got to make money to pay for the ones I already got." He reached into his pocket, pulled out three. He placed them into her extended palm and went back to tucking in his clothes.

"Will I see you again?" she asked.

"Yeah, baby. I'm always out there." He went to lean over the bed and kissed her lips. Savored the moment then walked away.

She laid all alone in silence. A few seconds later, the click sound of a door closing entered the bedroom. Remembering the crack he had given to her, she looked at them resting in the palm of her hand. She smiled to herself and reached out, placing them next to her clock while scooting out of the bed and headed toward the bathroom.

The water was just a little on the cold side. After making several adjustments, she stepped gently inside, pulling the curtain behind her.

Sonny Bee had sent Breeze out from his apartment to round up the posse. As he waited on the sofa thinking, there was a knock at the door. He rose, stretched his arms above his head and went to open it. Breeze led the members inside. The first ones found seats. The rest took up space around the wall. Sonny Bee looked directly at the group. He rubbed the back of his head with his finger tips. "I got a problem. Any help you can lend me would be boss."

"What you talking about, Sonny Bee?" asked Breeze.

"I got a small debt to pay. I need all the cash we can come up with in the next couple of days."

"You know we ain't big time," said Jesse, who was standing next to a wall, "but what's mine is yours."

"I can dig that and as a posse it should always be that way."

Everyone started digging into their pockets. Breeze walked around collecting all the donations. When the last man had given, he took a count. With a raised fist, he made his way to Sonny Bee shaking the dollar bills. "Here's $6,445 dollars. Here's help looking at you."

Sonny Bee smiled. Then it disappeared. "It's a help."

"What's with the cash?" asked Jesse. "I mean what kind of debt?"

"Believe me when I say it's for a good cause. I'll have to run it down to you in detail at a later date."

"Maybe you gonna surprise us with something?" asked Breeze smiling.

"If you say it's for a good cause," said Jesse. "It's O.K. with me. You been fair with me. It's my turn to pay back."

They all agreed.

"We still need to raise a little more, but I got an idea." All the member faces became blank. No one said a word. "Dig this. All the crack we got, we gonna double it by adding this powder." He went to the sofa, pulled out a small bag from behind it. It was half filled and white as snow. He passed it to Breeze while covering his mouth to cough.

"Check this out. I want all of you to break up your crack rocks so people won't be able to see the difference. Make it into powder just like the stuff in that bag."

"But that's cheating people," said Breeze, protesting.

"Whoever said dealers were fair people," Sonny Bee said. "It's how you play the game." He pulled a small capsule from his pocket, held it out for all to see. "We sell these rocks to make money or get high for free."

"Do you think we can get away with it?" someone asked.

"Yeah man. That's what most dealers do to increase their cash. You'd be surprise if you knew how many times this stuff was cut. There would be no way you could handle pure hits."

"Well, I'm down with you," Jesse said. "I'm saving to get me a new ride. I like the color baby blue."

"Solid! Then you guys are down with me, right?"

"Right," came a reply from the entire group.

Breeze placed the bag on the table. The rest of them came forth, placing their capsules to make one pile on the table. Sonny Bee went to work showing them how it was to be done. He showed signs of excitement and a willingness to do whatever it took to make money.

After yesterday's bust in Tower Two, the two police officers never got a chance to finish passing out the Mayor's fliers.

Today, they were out again in the single units. "The Mayor will probably have a fit when he finds out these fliers got out the same day he scheduled his meeting," said the White Officer.

"Maybe so, but taking those two into custody most definitely compensated for the lateness. He might even give us a pat on the back." The Black Officer patted his partner's back.

"Yeah, I bet. I hope he looks at it the same way you do."

"Why don't you try putting a smile on that face while you're working."

No smile appeared.

"Take that section," said the Black Officer as he pointed to a row of homes across the driveway. "I'll start in this section."

They split up. Both had their arms and hands filled with loose sheets of papers.

Breeze viewed his first lesson on how to cut crack. He was use to dealing with the full strength stuff. This weaker form didn't interest him. When it came time to pass it out, he passed it up. Some of the members joked about him refusing, saying he wanted money but he didn't want to work for it. In his opinion, if the stuff turned out to be bad, there might be problems for the posse.

Breeze decided to leave the apartment to go visit his mother who he hadn't seen in a couple of weeks. Even though their relationship was strange at the time, they still loved each other. He knew she loved him by the way she talked to him. She hated the neighborhood and didn't want him brought up in it. She often told him it made kids grow up too soon and destroyed the early learning process that children needed. Maybe she was right.

His father's house was only five blocks away. He worked on a low paying job, which prevented him and Breeze from moving up to a higher standard of living. Breeze would walk to Miller Homes every chance he got. This kept him in tune with his environment. All of his friends and his mother were here. His friends were teaching him the ropes of being street smart.

He began to climb the steps. On any normal day, he would race up them, taking the steps two and three at a time. But this time, because he was going to visit his mother, he didn't want to be panting for breath and sweating all over her during their hugging moment.

He reached the fifth floor a lot more winded then if he had run. Slowly he walked to her apartment, reading the creative graffiti on the walls. When he arrived, he tapped on her door with his knuckles. While waiting for the door to open, he looked around, taking notice that it was different up here. The floor was cleaner. Three working lights shined brightly in the hallway. But most of all, it was quieter. Just a low muffler of noise filtered in from below. Surprisingly, he could hear himself think.

Seconds passed. He tapped again. Suddenly, the door opened. A slender women, slightly taller than him, faced him. "Come in son'" she said holding a pleasant smile. "What a pleasure to see you again."

He stepped inside. Bertha gently closed the door. He walked up to her. She gave him a big hug. He kept his arms close to his side. Even though he didn't respond, she continued to hold him for a few seconds before his release. He felt good being with her. A smile flourished about his face as he made his way to the sofa to take a seat near the corner's edge. "How's things going Mom?"

"Oh, fair. I'm a little down since Butch was killed. But I'll be alright."

"Yeah, I was sorry to hear about him."

The room became so quiet they could almost hear each others thoughts.

"Are you hungry?" she asked. She didn't give him time to respond. "Can I get you some juice or maybe a soda?"

"No, I'm fine. I just felt the need to see you, to see how you were doing and all that." He walked to the sofa and seated himself.

"That was thoughtful of you. I'm glad you came. How's your father and how's he treating you?"

"Fine," he answered, keeping an artificial smile about him.

"One of my girlfriends said she saw you," she said in an excited tone of voice. "She couldn't believe how much of a young man you're getting to be." She started playing with her hands.

"That's cool."

She smiled in a surprising way. "What do you mean that's cool? That's great. I like it when people say nice things about you. It makes me feel good inside." She moved from the door and went to sit by his side. A worried expression crept over her face. "I hear you been selling drugs around here." Her voice became low and soft. "Is that so?"

The question surprised him. He lowered his head. "Yes, dad said he couldn't spare the kind of money I needed to buy good clothes and other things I like." He lifted his head to look toward her.

"Do you think it's right for you to take it upon yourself to make money illegally?"

He became excited as he jumped to his feet. "Mom, you got to understand that I'm fourteen. I'm not a little kid anymore. But I'm not old enough to get a real job. I got to do whatever is necessary. There's a world out there doing things for me."

She was totally surprised by his mannerism and the way he expressed himself. She sat silent for a moment, then spoke without raising her voice. "Do your father know what you're doing out in those streets?"

He turned his head to look in the other direction. "No, not that I know. He hasn't said anything to me."

"I think you should give it up."

He started walking around the room.

Her eyes followed him.

"Mom…"

She cut him short of finishing what he had to say.

"Listen to me son. Sooner, if not later, you're bound to get caught. Your friends can't help if they 're doing the same thing."

He stopped to look at her. "Some of them did already."

She became surprise to know he was still actively dealing even in the face of possibly getting locked up. "Oh, and what happened to them."

Breeze seemed more relaxed. "They got small fines. That was it. Oh yeah, a couple did a little time. I'm talking about one or two days. It was nothing to them."

"How would…"

This time he cut her off with a disturbed voice. "Mom, I didn't come up here for this. I came because I missed you and I wanted to see you. If I'm gonna have to go through this every time I come to see you, I might stay away longer the next time. Where do you think I get the money from I give you almost every time I come visiting?"

"I sort of suspected it was from drugs, but in my mind I didn't want to believe it."

"Okay, so now you know. I've come to learn that drugs and money go together. I'm broke right now and I don't have either. In a couple of days, I'll be back on my feet because I ain't never been down for long. I'll give you something then."

She continued to be surprised. "That seem rare to find you broke. I don't always expect you to come giving me money. If you ain't got it, don't worry, I'll survive."

He put his hands on his hips as he stared back at her. "You want me to stop selling drugs and at the same time give you money?" He dropped his hands.

She remained silent.

"I really have to be going."

"I didn't mean it that way, stay." She held out her hands toward him.

He didn't move.

She lowered them to rest upon her lap.

"Really," he said, "I do have some place to go."

"Don't go, you just got here. Let's talk a little longer."

He walked toward the door.

She followed. "When was the last time you saw your sister?"

He stopped at the door. She caught up to him. "About four days ago. She said if I saw you, to tell you she asked about you, and come visit when you can."

"That was nice of her." He opened the door wide and walked out into the hall.

"Don't forget to come back to visit. Please don't stay away so long son."

"OK, Mom. I promise."

She watched as he walked to the stairway and disappeared through the door opening.

Breeze returned to Sonny Bee's apartment on the seventh floor. Sonny Bee let him in. The posse had gone by now. Sonny Bee went to work on some wires behind his component set. Breeze walked to the window. Looking down onto the courtyard, he heard Sonny Bee speak. "What's up buddy?"

"Man, I just come from visiting my Mom. She had more questions to ask then Jack got liver pills."

Sonny Bee stopped for a minute to look at Breeze. "You should go see her more often."

"She was saying the same thing."

"Things wouldn't be that way if you did. She only wants the beat for you."

"I know. Don't you start in on me." He turned to face the room. The dog laid on an oval shape rug near the sofa. Breeze patted his leg. The dog came to him. He rubbed his head and the back of his neck a couple of times. The dog sniffed his clothes, and wandered away. "By the way, what are we going to do about Flash and his posse?"

Sonny Bee's head was buried behind a stack of elevated components, "A lot and so," he replied.

Breeze walked over to where Sonny Bee was working. "You keep saying things like that, but you ain't doing nothing."

Sonny Bee stopped working. He stood to give Breeze a mean look. "What you want me to do? I get mad every time I start thinking about him. I been looking for him and can't find him. Have you seen him?"

"Not since he jumped us. I think he's afraid to show his face." Breeze started walking toward the door.

Sonny Bee went back to work. "Where you going now?"

"Out, I got some place to go. If I see him first, I'll let you know where he's hiding out."

"OK, I ain't never seen a dude with so many ants in his pants."

Breeze laughed as he walked out of the apartment, down the steps and out of the high-rise into the blinding sunlight and blistering heat. Determined to take a short cut by going through the row homes section, he trespassed onto several lawns as he walked at a brisk pace. Suddenly, he heard a voice calling. "Hey you! Hey you, kid." He turned his head to see the Black Officer calling in his direction. Breeze stopped.

The officer walked up to him. "I got some questions I want to ask you."

Breeze showed a little anger. "I'm not a kid."

"You sure don't look like a man. I heard you was in the parking lot when the fight broke out."

"I don't know anything about no fight. There's fights out here everyday. I stay away from them. Most of the time, they just having fun. Who said they been fighting?"

"I know you know the ones I'm talking about."

"I was born half blind and I can't hear too well."

The officer gave him a stern look. "I can get tough on you. You're far from being an angel, act right. You don't have to snowball me. I know you know something. I want to hear it right now or would you like for me to take you in for dealing drugs?" He placed one hand on his handcuffs.

Breeze stopped to think for a moment, then he took on a real relaxed attitude.

"Yeah, come to think of it, I was in the fight. But I got away without getting hurt and I didn't hurt anybody. You can't blame anything on me."

"Besides from all that, who started the fight?"

"It was this dude named Flash. He has his posse with him. They stuck us up for money."

"Was a person named Butch in the fight?"

"No, he just happened to be there when it jumped off. He got robbed just like the rest of them. I know he got hurt because I saw a couple dudes busting him up real nice."

"Do this so-called dude named Flash live around here?"

"No, but you could say this is his second home."

"OK, you can go about your business, but if I see you selling drugs again, I'm gonna take you in. Do you understand what I just said?"

Breeze looked off in the direction he was traveling. "Yeah, I heard you."

"Alright, beat it." Breeze continued on his way. The officers watched his back until it disappeared from sight.

CHAPTER
Eight

The District Police Chief was talking with the Mayor on his telephone. "Yes Tom." There was a still silence about the office. "I got some people on it." The Chief seemed to be listening with extreme intensity. "Sure, that's the standard procedure. We file written reports on the Miller Homes situation as soon as they come in. OK, that sounds good, good-by." He returned the receiver to it's base and placed his elbows on his desk. He lowered his head between his hands and stared outward. "That man wants blood. I do believe he losing it."

A young black man walked into the Chief's office in street clothes. He was an undercover officer assigned to Miller Homes two days ago by the Chief himself to check on the ongoing drug activities. He closed the door behind him. The Chief looked up by lifting his head from between his hands.

"How's the undercover work coming along around Miller Homes?"

"People don't take too kindly to strangers. I sort of been hanging around there trying to get them to unclamp. Word has it, this kid named Flash had a lot to do with that gang fight and some possible involvement in a murder deal."

The Chief leaned forward. "Can we get anything on him?"

"I'm not sure right now. People who know members of his posse say, Flash and Butch had a run in over money."

"Posse?" said the Chief with overwhelming curiosity.

"That's what they call their group or now-a-day gang."

"Pull him in. I want him questioned. I got the Mayor on my back and he's riding hard. He thinks that place is a troubled time bomb waiting to go off. See if you can come up with something a little more concrete."

"OK, I'll give it my best shot." The plainclothes officer left the office.

Flash had not appeared around Miller Homes all day. He had money in his pockets. He was doing good by all standards, but he always needed more. On this evening, the sun was starting to set. This was a good time to go hang around Miller Homes, find some unsuspecting pray and perform a few stick-ups.

He headed toward Miller Homes on foot. As he walked through the courtyard and onto the parking lot, it became apparent to him that there wasn't as many people outside as normal. Some of Sonny Bee's posse spotted Flash. Instead of going after him, they took off running into Tower One and Two.

Flash continued on his way until he walked up behind an old man who had just stepped out of his car. The man had light grayish hair and looked to be in his eighties. He opened the back door, reached in to retrieve one of several packages resting on the seat. Flash tapped the top of the car to get his attention.

"Oh," said the man with growing large brown eyes. "You startled me." His voice had weakened through the years. "How you doing Sonny?" Flash didn't say a word. "Can you help me with some of these packages?" The old man wasn't as strong as he used to be. "I'll give you a couple of dollars for your service."

Flash had that mean look on his face indicating he was about to do something wrong. "Give me all your money," he said without hesitation.

The old man cupped his right hand around his right ear. "What you say Sonny? I can't hear too good."

Flash moved in close enough to talk directly into his ear. He balled one of his fist up tight and pushed it down by his side to show strength. "I said, I want all your money."

The old man payed no attention to that move but smiled instead. "Oh no, this little job is only worth a couple of dollars."

"Who's talking about work?" Flash pulled his pistol, stuck it quickly into the old man's ribs.

Feeling something hard against his body, he looked down. His smile died instantly. His eyes grew larger as he raised them to meet Flash's.

"This is the real deal, old man. Your life don't mean a thing to me, how you want it?"

Without giving it a second thought, the old man reached into his pocket, took out an old brown wallet. He held it up, but not straight out.

Flash pushed the pistol into his ribs a little harder and took a step backward. "I ain't got time to be fooling around. I'll take the whole thing." He snatched the wallet from the old man's hand and moved close to him again so he could talk directly into his ear. "If I hear of you telling anybody, and I do mean anybody, I borrowed your money, I'll be back to pay you a sweet little visit. And it won't be to bless your age. Do you hear me old man?"

The old man stood with his mouth dropped.

Flash removed the bills and started to walk away. Suddenly he stopped, turned and threw the wallet at the old man. It bounced off his shirt, causing him to flinch out of a daze.

The wallet made a dull thump against the asphalt. The old man bent to retrieve it.

Flash put his gun away and walked away.

The old man made no attempt to move from his position.

On Flash's way out of Miller Homes, he spotted a middle-aged woman coming toward him. When she was within touching distance, he grabbed her pocketbook from her hand. She reached out to grab it back, but Flash took off running and swinging it wildly.

"Police! Police!" she screamed. "Somebody stop him. He took my pocketbook."

Flash ran down the walkway and out of sight. The very few who witnessed all or part of what Flash did were kids, elders and a few stray drug dealers. No one made any attempt to go after him. Her screams became a sob.

Two of Sonny Bee's members had gone to his apartment with information that Flash was in the area. When Sonny Bee received the news, the three raced down the steps hoping he would still be there. But when they reached the lower level, all they found were the two people who had been robbed and a couple of kids playing. They decided to split up in search of him. They looked everywhere but he was nowhere to be seen in this area. Sonny Bee finally went back to his apartment.

The two members refused to give up. They went on to expand their area.

The meetings were about to get underway. Bertha had arrived early enough to find a seat near the front of the crowd. The Mayor entered the room shaking hands with residents. He managed to make his way to the front of the crowd and took a seat behind a desk facing them. While the crowd was talking among themselves, he took a moment to clear his throat. He raised his hand as a way to silence the crowd. When most of the noise has simmered down, he began to speak. "Today, I called this meeting to inform you that my office is taking further action to insure the safety and well-being for all Tenants of Miller Homes. Within a couple of weeks, this area will be fenced in with a few entrances." He stopped to look for objections. Everyone sat staring in his direction. "There will be police officers placed at each entrance to keep unauthorized people out. I know a lot has happened around here. I can agree with most of you that this area is unsafe with its drug dealers and thugs." The Mayor came to his feet, he leaned forward, planting his fingers firmly on top of the desk. "I plan to restore this community back to the safe place it once was."

"Alright!" Came a call out from an unknown voice in the crowd.

Bertha came to her feet. "Mr. Mayor, all that we have had so far is talk." The crowd agreed. She smiled as a sign of support rose in her favor from the crowd. "You say you want to cage us up like animals. Do you think this is the way to treat this problem?"

The Mayor stood for a moment in silence. "There isn't a lot we can do without your help. I was told that in the past, you Tenants have not been cooperating with the officers who are posted in this area. So, by fencing in this area, I feel you will feel safer even if you don't participate. With the presence of armed police officers in this area, I am quite sure we can bring most crimes in this area to a halt."

Bertha was not going to let the Mayor get off easy. "I can tell you why we haven't cooperated. The few dealers that have been arrested have returned to laugh at us. Some of them even had the nerve to threaten some of these Tenants." Another out burst of agreement filled the air. "These people don't want to get hurt because your system fails to punish those who do wrong."

An old man rose from his seat.

The mayor pointed to him as a means to silent Bertha. "Would you like to speak sir?"

"Just today I was robbed of my wallet by one of those kids. He told me if I said anything to anybody, he was coming back to see me. I can't live around here like this. He might hurt me the next time." The man took his seat.

A middle-aged woman jumped to her feet. The mayor pointed to her.

"One of them had the nerve to grab my pocketbook and run. I lost everything I had in there; welfare money, license, personal items and everything. It was terrible." She started to sob as she took her seat.

"Mr. Mayor," said Bertha, "while all this going on, it appears that no one came to their aide."

The mayor was quick to speak. It was a matter of saving face with the community. "This is just the sort of things I am out to prevent."

"It all sounds good," Bertha replied. "But I find it hard to believe you are willing to spend tax dollars in an area that has been considered a waste by many of your friends and associates."

Bertha moved to the end of the aisle. She walked to the door shaking her head in disbelief. "This is another political stunt," she mumbled. The mayor continued to talk about his plan. She left the room. Everything he was saying, had been said many times before. To her, it seemed the Mayor was stringing them along.

Bertha strolled across the parking lot. She spotted the dealer who had given her the crack. She waved for him to come toward her. He met her halfway between the Towers in the courtyard. They stopped and talked for a few seconds. Together they walk to her Tower, disappearing inside.

Sonny Bee sat on his sofa smiling about his accomplishment. In the past two days, his posse sold most of the mixed crack. Looking down at a hand full of dollars, he slapped the stack hard against his other hand. The sound made a loud POW. With this money he collected from the posse and the money in his nightstand draw, he had enough to get those goons off his back. It was indeed a cause to celebrate.

He went into his bedroom. Lit the same joint over again by taking several puffs before putting it out. It began to make him come alive. He was feeling good just being in a relaxed mood. Now that the pressure was off his back, this was a good time to go hang out with the posse and see what was happening.

He walked to the window. Pulled back a section of curtain hoping to catch sight of them. He could only see half the parking lot. None of them were visible. He would go down onto the courtyard looking for them. First he needed to get his pistol. This area was getting pretty bad. People needed protection. There was no way of knowing when he might run into Flash. Flash was a unpredictable character. Sonny Bee though it would be best to hide it somewhere on his body within easy reach. He pulled out his shirttail from around his waist and adjusted the pistol underneath so it wouldn't show. Then straightened his shirt so it hung naturally. "Better check it out in the mirror," he said to himself. He went to the mirror, took a long look. "Perfect Flash, make my day by appearing so I can blow you away." He liked the wording. It had a nice little ring. He pumped himself up to look bad. "Make my day by appearing so I can blow you away." A smile spread across his face as he walked toward the front door. He looked around, everything seemed cool for the time being. He went out into the hallway, locking the door and heading toward the steps.

Miller Homes provided no amusements for its children and young adults except for an old wooden sandbox, half filled with sand and a few empty beer cans. Children played within the confined area whenever the area was peaceful.

It was early afternoon. The day seemed calm. no wind was stirring and the sun was producing an eighty-five-degree heat beating against the grounds of Miller Homes. A small child, less than two years in age, sat half buried in the sandbox played unattended near the corner of Tower One with his legs spread to form a forty-five-degree angle. He used a broken handle, plastic, shovel to pour warm, dry sand into a bucket sitting between his legs.

Flash and six members of his posse walked out from an adjacent parking lot toward the Towers.

The child stood to brush sand from his legs and shorts.

Sonny Bee was alone. His posse had left the area earlier in the day.

As Flash neared Tower One, Sonny Bee appeared from within the doorway of the same Tower. They spotted each other around the same instant.

Flash's posse drew their pistols as they moved away in search for cover.

Sonny Bee produced his weapon while ducking backward inside the Tower. They knew war was on each other's mind. Neither side paid any attention to the child amusing himself as he played uninterrupted. The child sat again in the sand. He kicked his legs several times before throwing sand high into the air with both hands, displaying a fullness of vigor and cheer.

Without prior warning, Sonny Bee opened fire.

Adults, as well as kids, quickly ducked low as they ran for cover throughout the area.

Flash and his posse returned fire, causing a hale of bullets to create an unsuspected dead zone.

The child held the bucket up as if to display it for all to see, then poured the content between his legs. He placed the bucket to one side and applauded his accomplishment.

A gunfight had started to rag out of control. Flash's posse began to move wildly about the area in an attempt to get closer to Sonny Bee's location.

A younger mother started screaming, "MY BABY, MY BABY," as she ran out of Tower Two, not caring for her own safety and headed toward the sandbox. She seemed to race onward in a trance as the shots continued. Just as she reached the sandbox, the child was struck by a stray bullet, jerking him backward inside the box.

She stopped in horror.

The child lay motionless.

She gently stepped inside the box, staring down at the lifeless body. Blood started to flow from the baby's body outlining his circumference in sand with a dark reddish stain. With opened hands, she reached down and lifted the body to her chest. Held it dearly. Like a steaming locomotive starting to move, she begin to scream. Screams from the mother seemed to set off an alarm that cause the gunfire to trail off to a single shot before ceasing.

Her screams seemed to be the only noise in the midst of silence. Suddenly, she stopped, eyes glossy with running tears. His little arm and legs dangled lifelessly from its body as she slowly began to swayed him as if to give him comfort. A low sob began to release itself.

Members of the gangs took to running in various directions away from the area. People started coming from both Towers to gather around the sandbox. Sirens from far away started to grow louder as they raced toward the scene.

Bertha and the drug dealer were cracking it up in her apartment during the time the gun battle was taking place. She heard noises, but being at the height of her high, she nixed them off, thinking someone was playing with fire works. The two sat at the kitchen table, looking at each other. "I never thought for one moment that I would be talking against drugs in Miller Homes and doing them at the same time."

"You doing just fine, baby. I got some China Whites and Reds at my crib that will really take you on a journey."

"I'm game to try some."

"That's gonna cost you, you know that."

She laughed, he joined in. She patted the back of his hand that laid in the center of the table.

"You got that without even asking. You can have it in advance." They walked away from the kitchen, heading toward her bedroom. She entered first, he followed close behind her. The door seemed to close automatically.

The police arrived at the scene. The mother was still clinging to the lifeless child for dear life. Several medical people went to the sandbox to convince her to let the child go. A little at a time, she loosened her grip. The child was finally taken away and placed in a medical van. One of the medical aides helped the mother to her feet. He escorted her to the van. Once helped inside, the back door was closed and the van speed away with its siren blasting.

A few police officers started roping off the area. Other officers went about questioning Tenants pertaining to what had happened. A few witnesses came forth, naming some of the kids involved in the shootout. No one was able to give the name of the person who actually fired the shot, leaving the child motionless.

Many of those who stood around became outraged. Someone was saying that something had to be done and Bertha had been right about the Mayor doing nothing but talking over his head. Something had to be done before all of them either was going to get killed or severely hurt. It now boiled down to neither sex, nor age mattered in the war that was developing over drugs. A group got into their cars and headed toward the Mayor's Office. This would be the day they started their own war.

The drug dealers were sensing a war coming. Those who didn't own weapons, now was in the market to buy them through whatever means even if it meant going on a limb in finances. They could no longer count on safety in numbers to ward off rival members of opposing gangs. Each member had to be ready for that moment when it arrived.

The courtyard returned too normal. Dealers began taking their places in the parking lot. Among the crowd of dealers was a new dealer. He dressed in the style of clothing that most dealers wore and roughly looking to be of their age. He was the Chief's undercover officer. By strolling throughout the area, dealers became suspicious of him. On several occasions, he was stopped and questioned about his personal life and his community association. However, being the smart person that he was, he had ventured into this area several times to gain knowledge he needed to know to handle situations such as this. By keeping his eyes open and watching as much as possible, in just those few days, he had learned a lot. He was proud of himself. The questioning continued until they were satisfied with his answers. After a while, he was accepted. He was left to roam. He had convinced the gangs that he knew the ropes of dealing. That was part of his mission.

Cars came and cars went and so did people on foot. He became surprised by the amount of sales and friends he had made during the time he had been out there. The way people trusted him gave him a sense that this really was a business. Other dealers began to look at him in a strange way. He sensed something was happening. He decided to reduce his sales. It occurred to him that maybe he was making too much money. This was their territory and their customers. Trouble was the last thing he wanted. He went to lean against one of the Tower walls close to two guys. One of them had his back to the wall looking outward. The other was standing to his friend's front making hand movements as he talked.

The undercover officer placed his back up against the wall as he lifted one foot to act as a brace for his body. He moved a little closer to the two dealers who had their eyes on him. They kept their conversation between themselves, not caring about anyone's presence. The guy facing the wall started moving his body but not his feet. "Jesse, I don't know what's jumping off around here. Dudes going off left and right. It must be that stuff he used to cut this crack."

"It might just be, because I been catching word from some buyers that this crack wasn't on. I think we ought to dump it and go back to the good stuff."

Jesse looked over a capsule. "I know I ain't down with it no more. It's garbage. Did any of the posse rap to Sonny Bee about this stuff?"

"No man, I think they got cold feet. They're still hoping to pass it off."

"I'm ready to drop mine off at his crib."

A brown Chevy pulled into the parking lot. Three black teenagers appeared to be inside. The car rolled slowly as if the driver was looking for someone special. One of the dealers who recognized the car rushed up to it. It stopped. A teenager sitting in the seat behind the driver climbed out. He carried a mean look on his face and held a tight grip on a shiny baseball bat. The two talked for a few minutes. The dealer made a gesture to shake hands, but the teenager refused. In another movement, the dealer lowered his hand, placing it into one of his front pockets. He looked down in retrieving something. The teenager swiftly lifted his bat, swung it hard, hitting the dealer's face with the trust of a major leaguer. The dealer was lifted from his standing space as he fell to the ground. Quickly the teenager climbed back into the car and it sped away. Dealers close by began to gather around the fallen member.

The undercover officer looked on while holding himself back. He was use to getting into action, but he knew that all it took was one wrong slip up to blow his cover. He continued to lean motionless against the wall while mentally taking down the license plate number. When the car rolled out of sight, he walked far enough away so he wouldn't be seen using his cell phone. After completing his call, he walked back to where he was standing last.

The rest of the dealers were stunned when they realized what had happened. Customers casually walked away. Others drove off trying to avoid any possible trouble. Jesse and his friend went running to join the group. He couldn't believe what had just happened.

"Somebody call for an ambulance!" screamed Jesse. "This dude's dying. He needs immediate care." The only witnesses to the incident were a few dealers. None of them understood what took place. They ran off in different directions, not knowing whether to go for help or leave the area.

The undercover officer walked to the spot where the injured dealer laid. Part of his face had been smashed in. It looked bad. He returned to stand near the wall again. It was not his fight.

Breeze moved away from the crowd that had gathered in the parking lot. He didn't understand why anyone would want to do something like that. Maybe he would be better off not knowing. He walked toward Tower One. His old friend Scrap was sitting on a bench. He walked up to him curious about the drug bust situation.

"What's up Scrap?" he asked. Scrap held his head down staring toward the ground. He looked up to see Breeze standing to his front. "I don't know," he replied. Breeze sat on the bench next him. "When did you get out of jail?"

"Man," Scrap said, eager to talk. "I got out a little while ago. I learned a lot while I was down." Breeze straightened up. He became eager to listen. "Like what?"

"It was my first time, you dig. I was placed in this little cell, no bigger than my bathroom. It gave me a whole new outlook on life. I felt as though I was left in the world. I mean, time was passing me by and I was going nowhere. I tell you, all I could do was just sit there and either look at the bars or the walls. I could only take a couple of steps in each direction before walking into a wall or some bars. No radio, no television or any of that stuff. It was a bad scene. A total bust." Breeze looked surprised.

"You the first person I heard talk like that. Everybody else said the jail was filled and they got numbers with reporting dates." Scrap leaned forward again with a serious look on his face.

"Well for me, it wasn't like that. I got thoughts about doing a stretch over drugs."

"You sure sound like a changed person."

"Believe me, I am."

"Did they beat you like they do the dudes on television or them news riots?"

"No, but this dude associated with the prison system came to my cell. He was telling me about this program for first time offenders. He said if I choose to go along with their new program they're setting up, I won't have to pay a fine or go back to jail. You know what?" His eyes grew larger. "I'm gonna go for it."

Breeze thought for a moment. "What about the doe you could be making dealing drugs?"

"That's not for me. My future is going to come first from now on. I don't want my life moving like that." He stood, grabbed both pointed ends of his collared shirt, pulled them straight down and cocked his head to one side. "I wanna walk down the street with fine rags on my back, money in my pocket, people giving me respect and a job I can talk about in public." He released his shirt. "Drug dealers don't know about that. They work in the dark. Mostly behind closed doors, so to speak of, and secretly take unnecessary chances of getting busted. You dudes hustling out there in the lot is asking for the Knights to clamp you down. There's people watching you all the time. Sooner or later, the Knights gonna run down every last one of you, and the picture is gonna get pretty ugly. You dudes daring the Knights every chance you get. One of these times, you dudes ain't gonna make it back here."

"Man, they really did a job on you. All this ain't gonna happen to me. I got connections. Sonny Bee's backing me all the way to the bank. He's gonna help me get a car like his and some super fine chicks with money going to sleep. Someday, I'm gonna be the man."

"Sonny Bee ain't gonna be here forever. He can't watch over you day in and night out. If you keep dealing, someday you'll find yourself where I just left, jail. Or maybe like that dude who just got his face altered with the bat."

Breeze looked in the direction of the parking lot. "Is that what that was all about?" asked Breeze.

"Yeah, I heard about it all the way down in the joint about that garbage being passed off over here. I said to myself, somebody's gonna get hurt. My guess was right. I don't want any parts of it."

Breeze was constantly thinking while Scrap was talking. "I had a strange feeling something was wrong with that stuff, too. That's probably why I backed off."

Scrap gave him a strange look. "You know about that stuff?"

"I was there when he made it up."

"He went too far this time. Whenever this news gets back to him, he better be prepared to deal with it."

"He did it for the money."

I figure that. Look, I got'ta be going. I was just laying for the time being to kill some time and get my thought together." Scrap hastily walked away, heading toward Tower Two.

Breeze stood from the bench. He watched Scrap's back for a few seconds before running off to join the posse in the parking lot.

CHAPTER Nine

The Chief's two patrolling officers were in the single units checking on a complaint when they heard sounds resembled a car backfiring. They made no attempt to investigate because of the resembling sounds that were known to be taking place every day in this neighborhood. Un be known to them, a lone dealer spotted them out walking and set out to alert other dealers of their approach. As the word was being passed, dealers wasted no time in getting away from the parking area. A few went to gather in groups along walkways leading to Towers. The officers continued through the courtyard and into the parking lot. Out of nowhere, a young teenager ran up behind them. He appeared nervous as he spoke. "You missed everything. The whole police force was out here. A baby got shot in that sandbox over there." He pointed toward the area. "And a dealer got his face flattened with a baseball bat."

The two officers looked at each other in complete shock. "When did all this happen?" ask the Black Officer.

"Things around here never stop happening, you know that."

"That ain't what I asked."

"I guess in the last few hours."

"Holy smokes," commented the White Officer. "I know we gonna get burnt now. We're done for sure. The Chief finally got us."

The Black Officer frowned. "He can't do anything to us. We were on the job taking care of a complaint."

"Woo!" The White Officer put is hands in the air. "You don't know the Chief. He can do anything he wants, union or no union."

They ignore the teenager, but he was determined to fully inform them. "They just took the dude away who go hit with the bat." Neither officer looked in his direction. The teenager tried getting their attention by stomping his foot. "Hey! Do you guys hear me? Why are you never around when things happen? Where do you guys hide?"

The two officers walked away discussing the point that somehow there might be a loophole preventing them from getting fired.

The undercover officer spotted the two patrolling officers heading toward Tower Two. He waited until they had gone inside before drifting in their direction. He stopped short of the entrance. Instead of going directly inside, he leaned against the brick wall eyeing the area for any sign of someone watching him. Believing that no one was watching him, he started up the steps. The two officers went as far as the second floor. As they stood talking and looking through the window, they heard sounds of footsteps coming their way. When the officer rounded the stairwell, the other two officers stopped talking and the undercover officer walked up to them.

"I'm an undercover agent with the police force," he said. He took out an old black leather wallet with brown edging. Using both hands, he unfolded it. Sun light pouring through an opened window casted a reflection off the silver badge onto an overhead ceiling. A quick flicker of the badge's glare blurred one of the officer's vision. Realizing what was happening, he moved the wallets into the shaded area so they could get a better look. The White Officer gave a quick nod of approval. He folded his wallet and returned it to his back pocket. "That's the way I prefer it to be. If you see me out there, treat me the same as you treat them. I came up here because I want you to point out which one of those guys is Flash." He watched the White Officer move closer to him. "I can tell you right now he ain't here. At least

I didn't see him. He comes and goes like most of the rest. I don't think any of these punks live around here."

"I haven't seen him either," said the Black Officer.

"That don't matter. I'm going to be hanging around here all evening. If you see him, give me a signal or sign. I just want to see what he looks like. Don't get me involved. Is that understandable?"

"Can I ask why?" ask the White Officer.

"I'm on an assignment from the Chief. Let's leave it like that." The undercover officer moved back down the steps.

The officers watched him as he went to mingle with the dealers who returned to parking lot. The two went back to talking and scanning the area through the window.

A chauffeured driven police car put on its blinker just before turning into the parking lot.

"Look," said the Black Officer, "here comes the Chief's car. We better get out there." They moved down the steps and out onto the courtyard.

The Chief spotted them coming out of a building and had the car stopped.

The car stopped just inside the parking lot and dealers started walking away. As the two approached the Chief's car, he let down his side window. His face was red. "What the heck is going on around here? I sent you two out here to keep things under control.

Today we had one baby killed and another person put in the hospital. Talk to me! You better tell me something good."

The Black Officer became eager to talk. "Chief, this area is too big for the both of us to cover. We got drug dealers on one side, thugs in the middle and Tenants acting up on the other side."

"Don't you know how to call for back up?"

"Yes, but, things happen so fast by the time we zero in on it, it's over. And sometimes, more than one thing is going on at the same time."

"Do you need more help out here?"

The Black Officer's face took on a more serious composure. "Chief, we need an army out here."

The Chief let his window up as the car was driven away.

"Darn," said the White Officer, emotionally furious. "I don't think he's on our side. He didn't even offer us more help."

"Be lucky he didn't tell you to turn your badge in."

The White Officer began to remember what the Chief had said in his office. "Yeah, you're right." They walked back toward the Towers.

Bertha's girlfriend had finally gotten her hands on the marijuana. She knocked on Bertha's door. Bertha opened it to the length that the chain allowed. She stuck half of her face into the space to see who was there.

Then it closed again. The sound of a chain could be heard moving inside. The door opened. Bertha extended a smile.

Her girlfriend smiled back. With two fingers, she held up a small bag neck high, pointed to it with her free hand.

"I got it girl. It was hard, but my connections came through."

"Don't just stand there, come on in." Bertha's smile turned artificial. Her girlfriend was so happy to have the marijuana, she walked into the apartment with some jazzy steps.

Bertha shut and chain locked the door. Her girlfriend swirled around. "This stuff is better than others I had." She detected something wasn't right. Bertha had removed the smile from her face.

"Bertha, what's the matter?" she asked, showing concern.

"I didn't get any money from my son."

"That's okay child. You had me worried for a minute. Is that all? Girl, I'd trust you with my life. Pay me when you get it. Let's get this stuff cooking. I'm ready to get fired up." The sound of her words made Bertha laugh.

"That's only half of it." The smile faded from her girlfriend's face. "I graduated. I tried some crack and I like it better. It makes me feel a whole lot more alive." She spread her arms like she was conducting a symphony. A serious look swept across her girlfriend's face. She looked Bertha straight in the eyes.

"Girl, you're playing with death now. A lot of people dying from overdosing and others getting killed over it. Are you sure this is what you want?"

Bertha turned her back as she started walking around the room.

"I don't know." She stopped, turned to face her girlfriend and smiled. "All I know is that it makes me feel better quicker. There ain't nothing like it as far as getting high."

"I guess you know I ain't into that. I'm scared to death of it."

"It ain't no different from smoking that stuff in your bag."

Her girlfriend's eyes grew wide. "Oh yes it is. I've seen women trying to sell their kids to get more of it. Not only that, they'll sell their soul and gamble their life for crack. I can smoke pot until I'm blue in the face. Even pass out, but I know I'll be okay when it wears off. The habit from this," she held up the bag, "won't cost me anymore than ten dollars a day, but that stuff you talking about. It will take every penny you have everyday of every hour down to every second to keep up a good high, if you can keep it up."

"I know someone who will supply me with it."

"Yeah, I bet. You telling me somebody's gonna keep supplying your habit when it gets to be three or four hundred dollars a day?"

Bertha gave her one of those crazy looks. "I ain't that crazy about it."

"Believe me honey, it will grow on you like that. You should stop now before it overpowers you."

"I'm okay. I know how to handle it."

"That's what they all say. So, you're saying you don't want any of my stuff?"

"No, I'm gonna pass this time, but don't count me out. When I get tired of this, I'll come back to that."

"Crack is a one-way trip. I don't know of anybody who's left crack for marijuana."

"I'm gonna prove you wrong. I just fried some chicken. How about joining me for a bite?"

"You know, if I can't stop you on one thing, I can join you on another. You know I like your food because I can't cook."

They found that to be funny and laughed about it.

"How you gonna catch a man if you can't cook?" Bertha asked.

"I'm gonna charm him and sneak some fast food dinners on him."

"Girl, you're too much. Now I have really heard it all. Ain't that just awful."

They both laughed. "I feel sorry for the poor man and you ain't even found him yet." They continued to laugh while Bertha went into the kitchen. A few seconds later, her girlfriend followed, still holding the bag.

The undercover officer continued patrolling Miller Homes most of that evening waiting for Flash. The two patrolling officers had finished their tour and left the area. Being alone and without any inside help, he decided to call it a day himself. While walking through the courtyard, he spotted Sandy sitting on a bench with an odd colored dog on a leash. It was large, black all over except for its legs, which were completely white. During the past few days, he had been seeing her out here with this dog. If at all possible, he thought, she might be a possible source for information. He changed walking direction, guided himself toward her. She looked as if she was having a good time singing to the dog. He came to within ten feet of her before the dog noticed him and jumped wildly at him while still on his leash. Its bark was loud and vicious.

"Shut up!" Sandy screamed, and he obeyed. She went back to singing. "Beam me up Scotty, you control my body."

"Excuse me Miss."

She stopped, looked up at him.

"Why is your dog barking like that?"

"He don't like nobody. So don't think he's acting like this because of you. He only likes me and his master. I think you should keep your distance."

"I can see that, but first tell me something. Do you live around here?" Sandy hunched her shoulders.

"What do that mean?" he asked.

"I live here and there. It don't matter as long as I got a roof over my head."

"That's no way to live."

The dog laid down on the pavement in front of her.

"Who are you," she asked, "and what do you want anyway?"

"You can call me a friend of the people."

She stared at him. "And what do that mean? Are you a cop?"

"Do I look like a cop?"

She looked him over. "No."

"Lets leave it like that."

Sandy was so high on drugs she almost fell sideways from her sitting position. He made a forward motion to catch her, but the dog jumped up and started barking again, so he froze. She managed to catch herself and straightened up.

"Are you okay?" he asked.

"Sure, I'm doing great." The barking was getting on her nerves. "Oh dog, be quiet," she said in a more settle tone of voice. As he laid down, his barking trailed off to a complete stop. "What's your name?" She asked.

"Does it really matter?" he responded.

"Yeah, everybody has a name. I like calling people by their name. My name is Sandy."

"You can call me Pat."

She began to laugh.

"What's so funny." He asked out of curiosity.

"That sounds like a girl's name, are you?" She held her arm straight out like an arrow and began to move her hand in a way that expressed being feminine.

"No, I'm not queer if that's what you mean." There was a moment of silence. "How long have you been living around here?"

She looked up toward the sky as if to be stargazing. After seconds, she returned her attention to him. "I guess about two, maybe three years."

"Do you know most of the people in this area?"

She moved around abruptly. "What's this, twenty questions?"

"No, don't think like that. I'm just curious."

"I know quite a few people."

"Tell me, do you know Flash and his posse?"

Her face twisted up into an ugly expression. "That thug, I know him. I wouldn't give him the time of day." She leaned forward, almost falling to the ground. "Can I tell you a secret?"

He was eager to hear. "Sure, I have never given away a secret."

"Somebody gonna shoot that punk sooner or later. He's been robbing people left and right. Ripping off drug dealers and that sort of stuff. Some how I think he knocked Butch off. He didn't like him." She put on a sad expression. "He was such a good fellow." Suddenly, she perked up. "You seem like such a nice guy. Why don't I give you my apartment number. Come visit me. Maybe we can do some crack and talk. This dog won't be there. I can leave him with his master."

"I'd like that. So you do live in one of these apartment."

She responded with a smile while taking out a piece of paper and pencil from her pocketbook.

He stood motionless watching while she scribbled something down, balled the paper up and threw it to him. In a wild attempt to catch it, it bounced off his hand, but managed to catch it before hitting the ground. He looked it over and pushed it deep into his pocket. "Thanks, I'll take you up on that."

The dog moved into a sitting position in front of her. He sat peacefully and quiet.

"Is this your dog?" he asked again.

"No, I thought I told you he has a master."

"I'm sorry, you mentioned that."

"Don't worry about him. Like I said, he stays with his master most of the time."

"That'll make it more inviting to get me there."

She rose to her feet, slightly jerking the dog's leash, and it too, rose. They walked away together. Pat, as he was now called, could tell she was on something by the way she swayed a couple of times. He didn't know if it was the crack she had taken that was doing the talking, or was she really telling the truth.

The group of Tenants who had earlier piled into a variety of cars heading toward the Mayor's office was returning. The Mayor declined to speak with them. Unable to accomplish their mission, they decided to take actions into their own hands. Their plan was to set up teams and shifts to patrol the hallways in an effort to rid the Towers of all those who didn't belong there, mainly dealers and thugs who hung out on various floors creating mounds of trash and foul odors.

Furious, the Tenants displayed the anger felt by a lynch mob. They set up three groups of three man teams to be rotated and stationed in the two Towers. Within an hour, they had chased nearly twenty people away from the dwellings. Their next plan was to get some of the Tenants to volunteer to clean the hallways on each floor. And hopefully, they could get management to repaint the walls. This would have to be resolved at a meeting between the authorities and the Tenants. A special request would have to be sent to the main office.

The gang in the parking lot was a different story. It became obvious that the Tenants could not control them. The Tenants decided to put more pressure on the Chief in hopes of having him center more men patrolling in the vicinity of their area.

By the end of the first week, people who were patrolling the Towers didn't want to participate any longer. The authorities had not responded to their request and the police force didn't act on their suggestions. People who were chased out of the Towers sensed something had gone wrong with the Tenant's plan, started drifting back to their old hangouts inside the Towers. The pungent odors were returning and the trash was noticeably piling up on the floors again.

Breeze and Jesse were walking up the steps to Sonny Bee's apartment. They had just passed the fourth floor.

"Man, do this place smell bad," remarked Breeze.

"What you talking about. This is the same way it smelt before all that crazy stuff broke out."

"Maybe it's me. I've been walking through it so long my nose took a liking to it." They broke out into a chuckle. Breeze stopped to kick a soda can from a step. He watched for a moment as it rolled down to the landing and stop. Jesse never stopped moving upward. Breeze turned and hurried to catch up. "Jesse, did you read in the paper yesterday that the Knights caught that dude who busted Slim in the face."

"Yeah, that was crazy."

By now they were on the seventh floor. The two walked to Sonny Bee's door. Breeze knocked.

Sonny Bee opened the door halfway. "What gives me the honor of you two visiting?"

"A refill is in order," said Jesse.

"Why not come right on in" said Sonny Bee.

The three laughed as Breeze and Jesse walked in. Sonny Bee shut the door behind them.

"Sonny Bee", said Breeze. "That stuff you mixed was real garbage. It's a shame Slim had to go out like that. The paper said he died shortly after getting to the hospital. He didn't have a fair chance out there."

"That was the dumbest move you ever made," said Jesse. "We got Flash on our backs, and to add to that, now we got customers out there trying to pick us off, too. This stuff has got to come to a halt."

"I'm sorry about that," said Sonny Bee. "I'm not gonna be mixing anymore. What I'm giving you now is el premio." He kissed the tips of his fingers, and went into his bedroom. A short time later, he returned with two small bags. "Here's one for each of you. I appreciate the way you dudes got together and came through with the doe to get those hence men off my back. Someday your rewards will be great."

"We showed you where we were at," said Jesse. "Don't cross us up."

"Hey," said Sonny Bee, acting in a style portraying to be the God Father.

"You ain't got to worry about me. Before I forget, tell the posse to stop packing their rods. It's giving us a bad image. I saw some of the dudes twisting around their piece like they're some kind of cowboy. The next thing you know, they'll be shooting each other."

"I'll do that," said Jesse. "I think they need to be schooled on how to be cool."

"I'll tell them. Let's see what happens." Jesse led the way to the door. The other two followed. Only Jesse and Breeze went into the hallway.

The District Police Chief had his two patrolling officers from Miller Homes in his office. "We have a very serious problem over there," said the Chief. "People starting to get killed now." The Chief paced back and forth between them and his desk with his head titled slightly forward, while the two stood at attention. The Black Officer showed no signs of being surprised. "Chief, people been getting hurt and killed over there all the long. Nobody's been keeping score up to now because it's a black development. You know it's true that if it had been in a white development, this situation would have ended long ago. The FBI, CIA,

NATIONAL GUARD and Special Police Force would have all been there."

The Chief stopped, looked directly into his face. "Color has nothing to do with it."

"Believe what you want, Chief."

"I'm going to put two more men on to watch the housing section. I want you two to mostly stay in the courtyard area. But keep an eye on that parking lot. Maybe take a walk out there every now and than and see what you can see. I want some results, now go."

They left his office. Just as the door closed, the telephone rang. The Chief picked it up. "Yes, this is the Chief." There was a moment of silence. He lifted one end of the telephone cord, walked to the back of his desk and seated himself. "Okay Tom, I'm way ahead of you. I just assigned two more men to Miller Homes." A deep silence set in. He leaned backward to make himself more comfortable, but instead he became angry. "I don't have anymore men. Maybe you know something I don't." Tension was building up as pressure from the other end tried to consume him. Suddenly, he froze and relaxed. "Okay Mr. Mayor, if you want it that way. He sat straight up in the chair and slammed the receiver down. He mumbled a few words under his breath that only he could understand. Worried, he stood and started pacing the floor until finally going to the door. He spotted Bill sitting at his desk typing.

"Bill," he called. Bill immediately stopped typing to look up in the Chief's direction. "Get me six colored foot patrol officers between the ages of twenty-two and twenty-seven who haven't worked around Miller Homes. Have them report directly to this office. Then type up six sets of temporary orders. Make them out for an undetermined amount of days." He stopped to think for a moment. "Yeah, it shouldn't take longer than that. For the duration of this assignment, I want a patrol wagon and three more men assigned to it. As a matter of fact, have the patrol wagon's crew in here with the other officers so I can talk to all of them at the same time. And last, I want you to make out withdrawal slips for each of the six men in the amount of two hundred dollars in cash from our funds, under their names. You got that?"

"Got it Chief."

"I'm tired of all this running around. I'll handle this situation once and for all." His voice trailed off. "Yeah, I'll handle this once and for all."

Bill was still looking at the Chief. Sometimes the Chief had a habit of starting to talk again after telling people that was all. The Chief and Bill stared at each other. "Well get to it," replied the Chief. "I want all of them here as soon as possible." Bill walked to a file cabinet that contained folders on all the officers working in this district. Before long, he was able to extract six names of officers whom were on duty at the present time. He took the folders to his desk and began calling them.

Within an hour, all the officers were standing tall in the Chief's office.

"Men," said the Chief eagerly. "The reason I've gathered all of you." He paced back and forth across the floor in front of them. "Is because the Mayor can't take it anymore. Neither can I. The mess brewing around Miller Homes has to cease immediately. You know what this means. I have reassigned each of you to Miller Homes. Here's the plan. I want you men to go to Miller Homes in sets of two's in three unmarked cars arriving at ten-minute intervals. Park about a block from Miller Homes. Go on foot to where the dealers are. By the way, see Bill outside my office so you can pick up two hundred dollars. To continue with what I was saying, buy whatever drugs you can from down there. Don't spend anymore then a hundred and fifty dollars the first day. This is a two-day operation. Bring whatever drugs you buy back here. File a report giving names of dealers, if you can get one, and the amount of drugs bought. Act natural. Don't over play your hand. And no matter what you do, avoid at all cost letting them know you're a police officers. Report here tomorrow around 11:30 p.m. If you need assistance because of problems with drug dealers, ask either of the two uniformed officers to call the patrol wagon. It'll be stationed nearby."

He pointed to the patrol wagon crew who was standing off to one side. "That's where you three come in. As soon as they call, rush over to the parking lot and pick up whoever the uniformed officers have in custody. Bring them back here and have them detained. I'll take care of the rest. Any questions?"

One of the main six officers raised his hand.

"What's your name officer?" asked the Chief.

"John Holt, Sir." Holt was the oldest officer in this group. He was twenty-eight and had been on the force for the past seven years. He transferred to this district three years earlier after having several bad run ins with several white residents on his beat who didn't like blacks. He was told by his prior Chief that he could best serve the force if he worked around some of his own people. Holt took his advice. This is where he was sent.

"Speak Officer Holt."

"Sir, why did you choose us for this detail?" The Chief placed his hand over his chin for a moment then took it down. "I'll be honest with all of you. Foot patrol officers have a better repore with citizens. They learn to judge people through certain patterns. Constant contact develops. You know, respect builds on both sides and that sort of stuff. Most of all, the officer learns the street language and that's very important. I figured all of you would know how to deal with those Miller Homes people better then any officer who just rides around all day in his patrol car, or State Trooper whose main job is to travel roads. I hope that answers your question."

"It does, Sir."

"I want you to oversee this operation, Officer Holt." Just then an officer brushed something from his clothing. The Chief stopped to watch him momentarily. That motion set off a thought in the Chief's brain. "I'll call this, Operation Sweep Clean." The officer brushing off his clothing looked up at the Chief. "Yes," said the Chief, "Operation Sweep Clean." No one objected. "Do me a favor. Don't hurt anyone unless it becomes absolutely necessary. Those poor Tenants are about at the end of their strings. Go see Bill. Tell him I said give you three sets of unmarked car keys. Let me see some results. Go now, do your duty and help that community."

One hour later, Operation Sweep Clean went into effect. The first two officers arrived at Miller Homes in the manner they were instructed. To their surprise, there were many people standing around in the parking lot and nearby area. The sound of sirens coming closer could be heard from a distance. The first two spotted the uniformed officers in the parking lot.

By now, they realized something had gone wrong. They walked toward the two officers, excusing their way through a thick crowd that had gathered. When they reached the center of the crowd, they looked down to see two still bodies.

"What happened?" asked Holt.

"Police business," said the White Officer as he continued to take down notes. Holt tapped his shoulder. The officer looked up annoyed. Holt exercised his trigger finger for him to move closer to him. The White Officer tilted his head toward him. Holt began to whisper into his ear. "I would like to speak with you privately." The two walked away from the crowd. A short distance away, they stopped. Holt took something from one of his pockets, held it in front of him. The officer turned his head into different angles looking at what it was. They talked for a few minutes, then started walking back toward the crowd.

The second set of plainclothes officers came walking up. Holt spotted them. He managed to catch them before reaching the crowd. His partner just happened to be looking in his direction. Holt signaled for him to come toward them. When the four were together, he looked around to see if anyone was watching. It was clear because most of the attention was centered on the bodies.

"Men," Holt said, enthusiastically, "this is a bad day for us. It seems another gang got here about a half-hour ago. They tried to stick up the drug dealers. Someone informed the two patrolling officers that something was going on here. They came to the scene and was spotted by the gang of thugs. The thugs opened fire and the officers returned fire, hitting two of them for sure. The rest took off running. This area got shot up pretty bad. One of the officers said he would go through here to see if any of the Tenants got hit."

The White Officer returned to take Holt off to one side. They talked quietly, then Holt returned to his men.

"He was saying another plainclothes officer took off after some kid believed to be the leader. That's when one of them called for back up. They haven't arrived as of yet. There were two more officers in the housing section. They weren't called for fear of some possible activities starting over there."

By now, the last two officers had arrived. They came to join Holt's crew. They looked confused.

"It's over for the day," Holt told them. "Lets report to the Chief's office."

Nearly a half dozen police cars was arriving on the scene. The officers quickly got out of their cars and spread out amongst the crowd.

During all this time, the plainclothes officers were not noticed by the crowd that had gathered. After all, they were young, black and didn't look conspicuous.

Flash was able to get a full block head start on the undercover officer. The officer continued to chase after Flash until he was no longer visible. Finally, after giving up in an endless search, he decided to go to Sandy's apartment to pump more direct information from her about Flash. He made his way back to Miller Homes and knocked on her door several times. No one responded. He walked away. The day had been a real bummer. It was time for him to contact the Chief to give him a report. Knowing the Chief, he would blast him good if he found out from a second party about the blunder. No doubt about it, that's where he was heading.

CHAPTER Ten

Bertha had been feeling good most of the day. Her new male friend allowed her to go wild on his stash of crack. It was his way of getting close to her and at the same time easing the pain of Butch's passing. Everyday she managed to do ten to twenty cigarettes filled with crack.

At first it started out as fun and thrills, but now she was starting to feel the need for it. She only had two small cigarettes left. They lay on the kitchen table in front of her. She looked down at them confused. "Should I do them now, or should I do them later. Maybe if I do them now, I'll be much straighter later." She laughed to herself as she lit one. A jingling sound came from the other side of her door. It opened and her boyfriend walked in.

She laid the cigarette in an ashtray. "Honey, I'm so glad you're here. Let me give you a big kiss." She jumped up from her chair and went to him. He closed the door just as she put her arms around him. She kissed his lips. He put his arms around her.

"Baby," he asked, "you got something for me?"

"Sure, name it. If I got it, you got it," she answered. "Hold it. Let's do this little number I was just getting ready to blast off with."

"I don't have time for that everyday. I can't function like that."

"I can. I love it." Her face started to glow. She spread her arms out in an amazement of wonder. "I wish you could fill this whole room to the top with it."

"Me too," he said pretending to be fantasizing. "I could make enough money from one fourth of this room to quit hustling forever." He squeezed her tight.

She shook her bottom from side to side. "Would you really sell some of my stuff?"

He smiled a pleasant smile. "No baby, I couldn't do that to you." He let her go. They walked to the kitchen table.

She picked up the loaded cigarette. "If you don't want any, I'll do it all myself. I only have two. Could you give me a couple more?"

He took out six little tubes from his pocket, placed them in the center of her palm. She folded her fingers over them. The look on his face turned flat. "This is going to be it for a few days. Things are starting to get a little tough out there with those Knights always hanging around close to the parking lot. I might have to move to another spot if they don't go away soon."

Bertha's face straightened up. "Does that mean you'll be leaving me?

He looked worried. "I don't know baby. It all depends on how far I got to travel. You know I ain't got no transportation. Some days these walks over here can be a real trip."

She frowned, then changed it to a charming smile. "You better come over and see me."

He brightened up. "Baby, I can't let all that good stuff go to another man."

Each pulled back a chair from the table and took a seat. She lit a cigarette while taking a puff, then passed it to him.

"Here's to you." He took a deep puff, held it in, and passed it back to her, then lowered his head.

Flash circled the block several times until he was sure whoever was following him had given up and he finally made his way back to Miller Homes, up the steps to his Aunt's apartment in Tower Two on the sixth floor. After several knocks on the door, an elderly lady with grayish black hair, dressed in a flowery house robe let him in.

"Hi, Auntie," he said delightfully.

She didn't respond, just walked away toward the kitchen.

He strolled in, closing the door behind him. Instead of following her, he went straight to the front window. Looking down at the people below in the courtyard, they looked like large pawns from a chest board. "All those suckers," he said in a low enough voice so she could not hear him clearly.

"Did I hear you say something?" she called out as she stood over the stove stirring a pot.

Flash was not one of her favorite people. She was his mother's only sister with a willingness to put up with his crazy actions. Whenever his mother threw him out, he would come here, sometimes to stay with her. She didn't like it, but she accepted him because she felt she could at least talk with him enough to help keep him out of trouble.

He continued looking out the window, moving the curtains a little at a time. There was no answer coming from him.

"Flash," her voice rose a little louder. "I said, did you say something?"

"No, not really," he called back still facing the outside world. He let out a loud burst of laughter.

"That boy must be going crazy again. Every time he comes over here, his lips start moving and he says it's nothing, oh well." Just then, Flash saw Sonny Bee and Breeze walking out of Tower One. He straightened up. He pulled out his gun, took aim, waited a couple second,

"Pow, Pow," he said. "One for each of you." Then blew the imaginary smoke from the end of the barrel. Slowly he stuck the gun slightly into his waistband. "Boy are you two lucky this is my Auntie's apartment," still keeping his voice low. "You guys would make two nifty notches on my handle." He looked down at the handle. It had three notches carved on it. He lowered the pistol by his side and pulled his shirt out, stuck it into his waist band to cover it.

"There he goes again." His Aunt was not amused. "If I hear him answer himself, I'm leaving this apartment. "Flash!" She called loudly. "Get in here and eat some of this food. Maybe this will cool your brain down."

"Ain't nothing wrong with me," he called to her loudly. "I think everybody else got a problem."

"Lordy be," she said, while fixing his plate.

Flash walked to the table and immediately took a seat. She placed the plate in front of him. "What do you wanna drink?" she asked, making an effort to be polite.

Flash was starting to feel good and half-cocky. "Slow Gin would be fine." He looked down into his plate and began to eat with one hand and a fork in the other.

She tried to suppress a burst of laughter, but failed as it rushed out of her while making her way to the cabinet to get him a glass. She moved several pieces around until locating his favorite glass. Right beneath the cabinet, she began filling it inch by inch with cold water until it had nearly reached the top. She placed it to front his. "Close your eyes and concentrate while you drink this. It's gonna go down just like Gin."

He picked up the glass, looked closely at the liquid. "Yeah, anything you say." He returned it to the table. She left the kitchen smiling.

While sitting slump and starting to gobbling down large quantities of food, he noticed a picture of Miller Homes on the front page of a newspaper. He stopped eating to pick it up from a chair next to him. "Auntie, I see a picture of Miller Homes on this here paper. What's happening around here?"

"Everything." Her voice was low as if it was being muffled. "These kids done gone crazy, shooting, robbing and killing everybody. It's a darn shame."

"I thought this was a nice place to live. You got police protection and all that around here."

"That don't mean a thing. It's when you leave your apartment that the action starts. I don't want to talk about it anymore. It makes my skin crawl."

"Don't worry about the small stuff Auntie, I got your back." He put the paper down and went back to eating.

The District Police Chief was surprised in more ways than one when he returned to his office. First, it was filled with his newly created Operation Sweep Clean officers. And secondly, all the bad news they had for him. He walked around his office as he listened to the details. "Rats," he said, "this thing is worse then anything I have ever dealt with. It's like little Vietnam over there. Uncooperative Tenants and bad guys all mixed up together." He walked around to the back of his desk, pulled out a chair and took a seat. The men continued to stare at him. All of sudden, he jumped up as if the seat of his pants was set on fire. "I got it!" he said out of desperation. There was a moment of silence, and then a look of disappointment filled his face. "The mayor will have me put away for life if I do that. Others might call me a Hitler. On another hand, our only chance is to make out present plan work. Let's try it again tomorrow as planned. I guess you can all go for now." They filed out of his office. He stared at the closed door.

Sonny Bee stood in the courtyard surrounded by all his posse members. He felt a need to confront them. "As you can see, things around here are getting worse. We should all go back to carrying our guns. I know some of you never stopped. I got a new plan that will prevent you from getting robbed or trapped by the Knights. The plan is simple, work in pairs with one person protecting the stash."

"Good idea," said Breeze. "This means the dude holding has a chance to split or play it cool if something goes down."

Sonny Bee smiled. "I see somebody already got the picture. You dudes gonna have to decide who's gonna do what." He looked around at the members. No one had anything to say. "Okay, lets get it hooked up."

They split up into sets of two's, one person giving all his drugs to the other member. After a brief discussion, they set out to test their plan.

The rest of the day continued to move along smoothly until it became dark. Only a small group of dealers remained. They continued to talk, joke and horse play. Traffic rolling through the parking lot was starting to become very light. An occasional walking customer would drift in off the streets.

A few drunks stood around a bench near the end of Tower Two. They would get a little loud on occasions. They took turns pushing each other and laughing about it. One of them took a bottle from inside his shirt. He passed it to the guy standing next to him. He took a gulp while the others watched liquid roll from the sides of his mouth. Lowering the bottle, he wiped the liquid away from his face with his arm while passing the bottle off to the next guy who was eagerly waiting his turn. Impatiently, he waited for another turn at the bottle.

Several people sat on branches talking and watching children play while several young couples stood near the buildings talking softly. This night gave Miller Homes the atmosphere of living close to bliss compared to daytime activities.

The busiest days in the drug business usually started on Saturday afternoon and ran heavily through late Sunday night. This day was Saturday. All the patrolling officers around Miller Homes didn't work on weekends due to a manpower shortage and monetary budget running way over cost. Only a temporary detail could be assigned if the situation really got out of hand. At present, the situation was just that calling for his special crew.

The parking lot was filled with dealers. Cars lining up back to back. Dealers leaning inside car windows and buyers calling to them impatiently. All types of people walking around hunting for the best deals they could make. Dealers were making money.

The first of the two plainclothes officers entered the parking lot. A dealer just finishing with a nearby customer hurried toward them. They stopped when the dealer confronted them.

"Hey man," Jesse said, "I got the best stuff money can buy. You gonna like what I got. In fact, what I got is so good, you gonna wanna be my customer all the time and I want it to be that way. How many do you want?"

The two plainclothes officers looked around to watch some of the other dealers and buyers trading drugs for cash.

"We wanna buy some together," said Holt. "It's got to be what's happening and nothing less."

Jesse held out his palm. "Don't insult me man. I ain't got nothing but the best stuff."

"Lets see what you got that you think is so bad."

"I got nickels and dimes. How many do you want to buy?"

Holt folded his arms across his chest giving Jesse a macho effect. "You ain't showed me nothing yet."

Jesse got a little excited. "Hold it, don't talk to nobody until I come back." He flashed a finger in Holt's face. "Wait right here at this spot." He ran off toward a high rise. Seconds later, he came running back half out of breath with his hand extended, displaying his products. "Here's five nickels and five dimes. Take the dimes". He held them out while putting the smaller packs in his pocket. "I put a little extra in these. I want you to get a good one going. I know they will blow you away."

Holt looked surprised. He didn't touch them. "Is this all you got?"

Jesse became a little angry. "Man, I got all you want. You never said how many."

"Get five more dimes for my brother."

Jesse looked at Holt's partner who nodded his head in agreement.

"No problem," said Jesse, "I'll be right back." He ran off again.

Two more undercover officers walked into the parking area. A dealer immediately approached them. The dealers were determined not to let anyone leave the area without purchasing something.

Holt and his partner watched Jesse as he came running from the building just as before. "Here's ten," he managed to say between breaths. "This running can make anybody a track star. Maybe I should try out for the Olympics. What do you think?"

Holt smiled as he reached into his pocket, pulling out a roll of bills and peeled off five twenties. He looked up at Jesse. Jesse handed him all ten. Holt pushed the remaining bills deep into his pants pocket.

"Dig this," said Jesse, his eyes were almost wide enough to pop from their sockets. "All that money you got, I know you can burn a little more. How about it if I give you seven more for fifty?"

Holt thought about the deal for a few seconds.

Jesse began to push for more money. "Look man, you ain't gonna find anything better than this."

"No, that's okay. I got more things to do with my doe then spend it here. What's your name?" Asked Holt.

"Jesse. Everybody knows me. When you come around, just ask for Jesse. I'm here all the time. You gonna be sorry if you don't deal with me. I got'em. I don't make this kind of deal every day."

"I'll take my chances," Holt replied. "This stuff better be good."

"It ain't nothing but the best. After you do the first one, you'll be on. And you'll say 'damn', Jesse got some good stuff. I'm telling you."

"Okay, I'll take your word for it."

Jesse looked around and spotted two men looking his way. "I got'ta go. Got a couple of customers waiting." He rushed off.

Holt and his partner started walking away from the parking lot. "They're gonna be easy to bust," said his partner. "This is unbelievable how freely drugs move around here. They act like nobody's gonna touch them. It's a total free for all. A regular drug city."

"That's what people say about this place."

CHAPTER Eleven

Throughout Bertha's apartment, moaning sounds broke the silence. She lay on her bed balled up. Her stomach felt as if the inside were coming out. As soon as her boyfriend left, she went hog wild, smoking up all the crack, one right behind the other. They had gotten her higher than she had ever been. But now, several hours later, she was coming down. The withdrawal was getting the best of her. All she needed was just one more of those crack cigarettes to get her back into the swing of things.

"Oh God," she called out. "Don't let me die like this. I never thought it would ever get to be this bad." She managed to worm her way to the edge of the bed. Placing both feet on the floor and holding her stomach, she gathered enough strength to stand. She moved to a chair that held her clothes. Piece by piece she struggled to put them on, just barely standing. As she moved her body, the pain became less intense. It began to come and go in flashes. After the last piece was on, she decided to check inside her purse for money. Twisting and turning the contents, next to a book of matches, she noticed a balled up ten dollar bill showing. She took it out. Pulled it apart. Three more tens were there. Her eyes grew wide. She didn't remember ever having this much money. Not in her wildest dreams could she imagine where the money came from. She felt the pain again, but it didn't hurt as bad now. Her thoughts were directed somewhere else. "Yes! I could get enough crack with this to keep me going for at least a couple of hours." Then something clicked. This money was to be used to buy food. She stood thinking for a moment trying to decide which one she needed the most. Finally, she gave up. It was time for her to head for the parking lot. She finished preparing herself by patting her hair with the palms of her hands.

Bertha made her way out the door and started down the steps. The pain began to eat away at her. She had to stop to rest. After a few seconds past, she took a couple of deep breaths and continued downward. Upon reaching the third floor, sounds of people talking began to come through an opened doorway.

"Man!" I'm the one that's holding." Bertha stood in the doorway looking down at the teenagers sitting next to each other on the floor with their backs half turned to her. One teenager was holding something long and slender in his mouth. He quickly jerked it out of his mouth and out of reach from his friend.

"Cool it. You'll get your turn. A man can't even get a good hit without you acting greedy." He returned it to his mouth.

"Who do you think gave you the money?" asked his friend angrily. He folded his arms across his chest. "Do you think the stuff just fell from the sky into your hands?"

Bertha hit the side of the door frame with the side of her fist. The two stopped arguing to look back at her. She walked in closer to them. They didn't try to hide what they were doing. Bertha held money out for them to see. Neither one of them took noticed. "Can I get a hit off that? I could really use one." She had a sad look on her face. The two teenagers looked to one another, then back to her. One of them leaned forward. "Do I know you?" he asked. The other teenager squinted his eyes at her, and raised a finger to point in her direction. It shook several times before falling into his lap.

His partner laid back to rest his head against the wall, his eyes appeared to be almost closed. "Yeah, he said, bringing his half opened eyes up to meet hers. He was so high, he could barely see. "You that broad been at those Mayor's meeting talking against us."

She stared at the kid. A guilty feeling caused her body to go partly limp. "Not anymore. I've found the finest thing in life and I'm down with it. I really would like to get just one little hit."

"This is surprising news to me," said the one still holding the joint. "You really had me fooled, everyone else too, including the Mayor. You know, you got a decent rap. I like that in a woman. You sure know how to stick it to them when it comes to talking." He waved his hand for her to move closer. "Come on. You can get down with us." Bertha pushed her money into her pants pocket.

His partner objected. "Not yet. It's still my turn."

"Okay, that's cool. Get yours and pass off to her." They broke out into a burst of laughter. Bertha failed to see anything funny in their remark. It must have been some kind of private joke. Her smile was mixed with pain as she moved closer to join them. After the other kid had taken his turn, he passed it to her. She was so eager to have it, she almost coughed while taking a drag. Within seconds, her high started making her feel better. The pain was going away.

"Can I buy some of this from you?" she asked. "This is just what I needed. I got money." She started to reach into her pocket. One of the teens shook his head in denial.

"Really, I got money, she said still reaching for it. "Here."

"Hold it," he said raising his back from the wall to make a no jester with his hand. "We got enough for ourselves. You can get all you want down at the lot." She took an empty hand from her pocket.

"Thanks for the puff," she said with delight, still holding the joint. She took another puff and passed it back. She turned away and continued on her journey toward the parking lot.

There were a few scattered clouds in the sky as she stepped out of the building. This was one of those hot days. Business in the parking lot had died down. Bertha's eyes searched the area. She caught sight of Breeze with a group of dealers standing near a parked car. "Breeze," she called. He didn't respond. "Breeze," she called again. This time he turned in search of her voice. She waved for him to come. He ran to her.

"Son, I need something from you."

"I ain't got much money," he said looking helpless. She had a serious look about her. "Son, listen to me. I got forty dollars. I want you to take this." She took the money from her pocket, placed it in his hand. "Get me as much crack as you can with this. You know these kids. I'm sure you can get a good deal from them."

Breeze's mouth dropped open. "Mom, what you buying this stuff for? That stuffs drugs."

"I know what that stuff is. Don't worry, it's for a friend of mine," she lied. "Now hurry. Do as I say and stop looking like that and asking questions"

"I don't know Mom. You look like you're loosing weight. Some of the dudes say that's a sign of people on drugs. You starting to look a little pale, too."

"Never mind all that. That's because you don't visit me like you should. People's weight never stays the same. It's my eating habits that I've developed."

"This ain't for you, is it? Tell me the truth."

She looked straight into his eyes. "Just do as I say. Why you asking me all these questions?"

He hesitated for a moment, and ran off into Tower Two. A couple of minutes later, he returned, giving her what he received for the money. She took it, never thanking him and went back into her high rise.

Breeze stared at her building even after she had gone inside. After a few minutes, he ran back to join his friends.

It was just three days ago that the Chief mapped out his plans of strategies on how the men should make their approach in capturing the drug dealers. Again today, with Officer Holt as their leader, the group was ready to make their bust. The crew had just parked their cars two blocks away from Miller Homes and was proceeding on foot. The patrol wagons were increased to three. They were stationed one block away from the parking lot just as before. The men split up to cover certain areas. At five-minute intervals, they arrived at the parking lot. The same dealers as before came running to them for more business. It was Holt and his partner's job to keep things under control until everyone was in place.

When the last of the officers had arrived, everyone purchased more drugs and joked with the dealers. All of a sudden, Holt pulled out a pistol.

Jesse looked at it with greed. "Do you wanna trade it for crack?"

Holt made no comment. He fired twice over his head. The other officers pulled their pistols and fired once. This was an act to show support to the leading officer.

This established an invisible perimeter around the dealers. Everyone within the circle began to run in mass confusion around cars and into each other.

"Halt!" Shouted Holt in his loudest voice. "This is the police. Don't do anything foolish. You are all under arrest."

Everyone stopped moving. The officers began to move the crowd toward the center of the parking lot. Holt removed his walkie-talkie that had been strapped to his body beneath his sweater. He called for the patrol wagons.

While the wagons were in route, the dealers and buyers were separated into groups. With dealers being searched first. Three officers did the searching while other officers watched with trained eyes. Shortly after the wagons arrived, the two Miller Homes officers, who had been instructed to stay out of sight until the wagons arrived, now came forth. They joined the other officers in acting as part of the team. Together, they helped placed all the dealers in available wagons. All the customers standing in a separate area were divided into small groups and carried away, one group at a time. Tenants began coming from all the Towers and headed toward the parking lot to observe what was taking place. They cheered as each wagons drove away thinking their problem had been solved.

Some time later, the wagons arrived at the detention center. All the arrested were led from the wagons to holding cells. The bust had netted a range of dealers from ages, eleven to nineteen. They played the bust off as if it was one big joke. They horsed around in the cells, playing, pushing and pointing at each other.

One by one, the dealers were taken away to be processed. Every time an officer came to their cell, he was called names and laughed at. The officer remained calm. He didn't speak to any one while transporting them to and from processing.

CHAPTER Twelve

The Chief was in his glory. This was a great day for him. He had solved his most depressing problem. All the officers involved in Operation Sweep Clean stood before him in his office. He sat on the front edge of his desk.

"Men, I am extremely proud of you. The operation went off extremely successful. Not even one person got hurt. That's a sign of professionalism. I'm sure the Mayor will be proud of you men, also." The telephone on his desk rang. The Chief picked it up. He was in a cheerfully good mood. Even the small smile he wore on his face set off a glow.

"Hello, this is the Chief." There was a brief silence. The officers smiled as they looked around at each other. While the Chief listened, the expression on his face started to change.

"What do you mean? They are all back out on the streets." The officers lost their smile. "And you say the jail has exceeded its capacity with more serious criminal offenders?" The Chief began to express anger. "Why don't we turn the whole city over to those people." He slammed the receiver on its base. The whole room became so quiet you could hear yourself think. "Men, I guess you overheard part of the conversation. I have been informed that the jail is overcrowded. In fact, the jailhouse has until midnight to get rid of thirty more to prevent being fined." He rose to walk back and forth in front of his men. With dignity, he looked at each of their faces. "We did what we had to do. You did the best we could. You did a fine job."

The group of drug dealers walked along the street heading toward Miller Homes. As they moved along, they boasted about what they did when the bust took place and the way they gave the police officers a hard time during processing.

"Dig man," said Jesse. "I'm gonna get that dude. He ripped off my whole stash. All my scratch, and my piece." He kicked hard at something on the ground in front of him. It sped away. "Damn, my piece, too. That was a bad piece. We got to get more guns."

"And dig this Jesse," said Breeze. "They told me I was just kissing butt to some king pin. I should be lucky he didn't make a punk out of me. I laughed until he told me to shut up." Everyone started laughing out loud. Breeze stopped walking. "And dig." Everyone stopped to look back at him. "They had the nerve to ask me who I was working for." He threw up his hands. "Naturally, I said." He made an ugly face. "Your Momma." The group broke into another roar of laughter. Some of the guys were holding their sides. "You should of checked out the changes on their face. They said I was lucky I wasn't just a little older. I could tell they wanted to break my face."

Moving along, they finally walked into the parking lot. Some of their boys were there to greet them back. The group started telling everyone about what had happened.

Tenants who view the returning group lit up in surprise. They looked at each other in disbelief. Several of them got together and talked quietly. Their small group began to show signs of anger. Everything Bertha had said at the Mayor's meeting was true. She had even predicted the dealers would be back on the street shortly after being arrested. They would have to act on their own now. "We going to the Mayor's office," shouted Harry as loud as he could. "Anyone willing to go with us as a show of hands is welcome."

Harry was the type of person who mostly kept to himself. When something interfered with his way of life, he was known to take action. This had become that situation with the gangs of evil doers. A few more Tenants joined the small group which made Harry seemed pleased.

George was one of Harry's long time friends. He looked straight into Harry's eyes. "Let's get Bertha to be our spokesperson."

The whole group agreed.

Harry thought for a few seconds. "Good idea," he replied.

The group left, heading in the direction of Bertha's apartment. They only had to knock once before Bertha opened the door, dressed in a robe. Harry, standing in front, removed his cap. "Bertha, we got problems and need your help," he said in an angry voice.

I ain't feeling good at all," she said in a weak voice. "I doubt if I'm able to help anyone. That's including myself." She turned her eyes away, looking down toward his shoes.

"The dealers are back," he stated. "We need someone like you who ain't scared to voice an opinion. We want you to go with us to the Mayor's office. He's got to do something about these drug dealers before all of us get hurt or even killed."

She kept her head titled forward and began to lean on the door's edge. "Like I was saying, I'm sick and can't do it. Don't try squeezing blood out of a beet. I'm just not able."

George seemed depressed. "Okay, we'll have to do it ourselves. You take care, you hear."

She nodded and Harry led the group away. Down the stairway they filed, out of the building and across the courtyard toward their cars.

The dealers observed them coming toward them. "Well," said one of the dealers. "Look what we have here. A flock of chickens running for their cars."

People standing within the parking area broke out in laughter at the remark. The dealer's eyes followed the Tenant's movement. "Do you Tenants plan on making a move soon?" One of the dealers called out.

No one said a word. The laughter became light. "Getting pretty hot around here, ain't it guys?" said another dealer. They made sounds of agreement.

The tenants continued walking as if not to hear or see them.

The dealer was gaining support from other dealers by now. "Maybe the cat's got your tongue." He pointed his finger in the group's direction. "The next time all of you set us up, we gon'na have something for the bunch of you. Walk soft and don't make any waves. Don't you ever forget it. This is our territory." He quickly pointed one finger to his chest and his other hand toward the gang members. "Our territory," he shouted.

By this time, these Tenants had reached their car. Other Tenants had been sitting inside their cars waiting for others to return from Bertha's apartment.

Harry stood by his opened car door with his back facing the speaker. He turned to face him. Harry held a stance of self-pride. The rage within was visible. "Your days are numbered. You guys are really something, thinking we gonna just let you run over us like we are nothing. You'll leave this area one way or another. Another it will probably be."

Some of the dealers gave him the finger as they moved closer together, heading toward the Towers.

Several cars pulled away heading toward City Hall. When they arrived downtown, all the cars parked in a pay lot close to the building. They filed out of their cars. Everyone came to where Harry was standing. Together, they walked one block to City Hall.

Upon entering the building, a uniformed guard stopped them. Harry told him where they wanted to go. The guard pointed to a stairway and gave them directions to where they should be going. The stairway led to an upper level within the building and into a slightly congested hallway. Harry and several others looked at the names and titles on several doors as they made their way through the area until finally reaching Mayor's door.

Harry grasped the doorknob. George, who was directly behind him, grabbed Harry's arm. "Are we sure this is what we want to do as a group?"

"You got cold feet or something?" answered Harry. "If you're afraid to talk with him, I'll do the talking. I'm tired of their mess, too. Ain't that why we're here?"

George didn't speak. He let Harry's arm go and Harry turned the doorknob, but before the door could fully open, George was quick to touch Harry's hand. "I'm not backing out," his voice was low. "I'm just trying to make sure all of us are together." He let Harry's hand go.

Harry took a look at the group. Most of them nodded their head, meaning the group was still together and in agreement.

George slowly released air within his lungs. "Let's get on with it. I'm burning up inside."

Harry opened the door and the group filed in with the last person closing it. A secretary, working at her desk, glanced up at them. After seeing so many people, she stopped typing. "May I help you with something?" she asked. Her voice was soft and pleasant.

"The Mayor," Harry said with anger. "We wanna see the Mayor."

She didn't let Harry's harsh words detract her from being calm. "What might it pertain to?"

"It's them freaking drug dealers. They've taken over our Miller Homes and we want to see the Mayor about it. Right now, if you don't mind."

She placed the phone receiver to her ear, pressed a few buttons with her other highly polished set of long fingernails. As she sat waiting to hear a voice on the other end, she stared into Harry's face as if she could read his expression. It was the sign of a worried aging man with deep receding hairlines. "Mr. Mayor," was her sudden response into the receiver, "I think you have a real problem out here. My office is filled with people. They say are from Miller Homes. May they come in to see you?" A few seconds passed. She pointed to his door. "Go in through there and he'll see you now."

Harry wasted no time in taking the leading.

The Police Chief parked in the City Hall's employee's parking lot section. He made his way across the street and up several steps into the main lobby of the building. He waved to the guard in passing. They exchange silent greetings as hand jesters. Finally, he came face to face with one of several elevators and pressed the upward button. He watched as a lit number above the closed door moved from three to two and finally one. The door opened. Three ladies stepped out. He entered alone and immediately pressed a number button. The moment the door closed, the enclosed platform jerk upward until reaching the selected floor before stopping and he exited. Not sure of which direction to travel, he looked in both direction and proceeded in the direction he thought was the Mayor's Office. Two men, walking side by side, passed him going in the opposite direction like he was invisible. He came to stop at the Mayor's

Office. Wasted no time in opening the door. A secretary sat at her desk facing anyone who entered the room. He walked up to her desk. She looked up, taking notice of him, smiled and stopped typing. "Well, well, if it isn't the hard working Police Chief."

He smiled also. "It's hard work and tough. Can I see the Mayor?"

"He's got company. Lots of company."

"Do you think I can get to see him sometime this day?"

Her smile grew stronger. She changed her sitting position to lean back into her chair. "I don't know. Let me ask him. He's with the people from Miller Homes."

His eyelids lifted. "Good, that's why I'm here. Don't bother to call him." He gave her a big smile. "I know how to let myself in." He immediately walked to the door.

Her smile disappeared as she jumped straight up from her chair. "You can't go in there."

He quickly turned the knob. She moved away from her chair toward him, but not fast enough to catch him as he ducked inside and closed the door behind him. As if to be struck by the wave of some paralyzing force, she stopped moving.

The Mayor stopped talking in the middle of a sentence when he saw the Chief. He directed his conversation toward the Chief. "I'm glad you're here. We still have serious problems around Miller Homes."

The group of Tenants were so quiet you could almost hear them breath.

"I know Mr. Mayor. The Judge released every one of those dealers I had arrested. I plan on seeing him next when I leave here."

Harry began to look a little worried. "What's happening with the Say No Task Force? And I thought you was gonna put a fence around Miller Homes."

"We are," said the Mayor. "It just takes a little time. This involves a lot of paperwork to be pushed through channels to get the necessary funding. Believe me, I'm pushing."

"Bertha was right," Harry remembering her words. "From the way you're saying things, it sounds like most of us might have to die before this thing is approved. You got to understand we want something done right now, not tomorrow. We would appreciate seeing some action."

"Okay, I'll put all the pressure I can on the Governor to keep things moving. There's nothing around here any of you can do. It's all legal work." The group showed signs of being disappointed. "Why don't all of you go back to your homes for now. I promise you I'll take care of it as soon as I finish with the Chief." The Mayor began to look a little worried at this point. "Please, one of you call me in about two hours. By that time, I should be able to give you some information on whatever progress I've made." The chief watched as the disappointed Tenants filed out.

"Tom," said the Chief as he leaned on the front of the Mayor's desk. "We got to do something about this situation. The jail's filled and unable to handle anymore bodies. This is so degrading."

"I know. I promised those people I'd make life better for them over there. And now I can't even lock up the troublemakers. Let me call the Judge right now." He dialed the number. "This is the Mayor. Let me speak with the Judge." There were a few seconds of silence. "Okay, thank you." He hung the receiver up and looked up at the Chief." "Darn, the Judge is holding court at this moment. One of the secretaries did say she'll have him return my call after the case he's hearing is finished."

The Chief started walking around the room. He stopped near the window.

"Tom, you know, I've been thinking and I don't know what to do. I'm really lost on this one."

"Are there any police officers patrolling that area now?"

"No, I had all of them taken out after the final stage of that drug bust. I only had a few men to spare in the first place. They couldn't cover a territory like that and do a decent job. There's just too many obstacles. Everything down there was starting to go haywire. I'm surprised that some of the Tenants came to you for help."

The Mayor leaned back in his chair. "I'll give you a call later. Maybe I can get the Judge to do something."

"I hope so." The Chief walked out of the room.

Pat was picked up with the bunch of dealers during the drug bust. He stayed with them in the holding cell playing it up to the maximum. When he was taken away for questioning, he revealed his identity only to them. They checked it out. Word came back that he was to be cleared and returned to the group.

Shortly after the gang arrived in the parking lot, Pat showed up, hoping to find more clues that would be of help to the Chief. He leaned on the side of a parked car observing the dealers talking in small groups.

One of Sonny Bee boys spotted a small group of teens coming toward Miller Homes. He stared at the group. "That looks like Flash's posse," Jesse called out in a disturbingly way.

"That is," another was quick to cry out. "I'm gonna get my piece. I want him for myself."

"Not if I get to him first," said, still another. "My piece is still in my apartment and I'm on my way, see yah."

The whole group took off running toward the high rise buildings. Pat moved close to a building, making it harder for Flash's boys to see him. He waited until they had gotten close to the building before running three quarters of the way around it so he could come up behind them. This would place him in a position where he would be on the inside of the courtyard, nearing the building's edge, he stopped and placed his back flat against the wall. He moved his head in jerking motions, looking around the area facing him. He changed his position so to have his stomach facing the wall. Then moved closer to the edge to get one eye looking around the building's edge.

Flash and his posse stood in a bare space within the parking lot that was large enough for five parked cars. He talked to his men. "You saw them scattering like a bunch of roaches. They talk bad, but you see where their heart is."

From where Pat stood, he was too far away to pick up Flash's low speaking voice. Suddenly, the posse spread out, leaving Flash standing alone. Pat eased to within a fifty feet of Flash, drawing his pistol and taking direct aim at him. "Flash!" he called out. "Put your hands straight in the air. As high as you can get them. Move them quickly."

Flash turned to see who was there before doing anything. Pat brought his other hand up to his pistol for support. "Tell your boys not to shoot. If they go so far as to fire one shot, I'll shoot you down."

Flash was in no position to be bargaining. Pat was a total stranger to him. None of the gang members from around this area knew him. Flash thought it was best to obey the given command. "Boys, don't shoot. He looks like he means business."

The members stood their ground waiting to receive the next command.

"I'm taking you in for the murder of Butch."

"You got to be joking," Flash said surprisingly.

"Pull your hands down to your waist, keep them in front of you and walk this way." Flash came to him and Pat pressed his pistol against Flash's chest while using the other hand in an attempt to tie Flash's hands together.

Meanwhile, Sonny's posse came charging from the Towers and spotted Flash with his back turned. Without hesitation, they opened fire. The first bullet struck Pat's shoulder on the same side he was holding his pistol. Pat dropped to the ground, letting the pistol fall free from his hand.

Flash wasted no time in running around a corner to safety. His posse ducked down low and began to return fire.

Bullets bounced off brick walls. Windows shattered and people screamed as they ran for cover under benches, inside building and behind vehicles.

Pat managed to retrieve his pistol and crawled around to the side of one of the Towers. His vision came to focus on Flash, who was dodging through parked cars on his way away from the action. Pat managed to raise his pistol in Flash's direction only to find there was no way to get a clear shot. He was not a lefty, and therefore, his shooting ability was poor. He lowered the pistol without firing a shot.

The gangs continued to fire at each other until they ran out of ammunition. Flash's posse took off running down the street while Sonny Bee's posse retreated into the Towers.

Pat managed to lift himself from the ground to his feet. It wasn't a serious wound, nevertheless it didn't look good either. He lay against the building for several seconds trying to compose himself for what he had to do next. All the action had quieted down except for the sound of cars moving along the outer street limits. He walked away from Miller Homes.

People who had ran for cover inside Towers were now beginning to come out and ran in different directions.

Jesse and the posse ran to get more ammunition. When they returned to the courtyard, all activities had stopped and a still quietness gripped the area. Jesse called the posse members to gather around him. He looked disturbed. "I think it's time the posse fell under new leadership. We really ain't got no leader."

"What about Sonny Bee?" someone said.

"Yeah," Jesse was quick to respond. "What about him? He ain't never with us when things jump off. Like the gun battle, the bust and us getting hit with the rip off. He just likes to show off."

"How we gonna get any drugs?" asked another member. "He's got all the connections."

Jesse stuck his chest out. "No he ain't. He might have a lot, but he don't have them all." The posse stared directly at him. "I got some, too. I know I can do a better job than Sonny Bee. I want to be your leader. I can get just as much as he can, if no more. Besides, you dudes need somebody who's willing to go down with you every time something jumps off. Ain't I been down with you all the way?" He looked around at each member of the group. They agreed.

Just then Sonny Bee's candy red Jaguar pulled into the parking lot. All the gang members except Jesse looked a little scared. No one said a word. They watched as Sonny Bee parked his car. He and Breeze stepped out. They started walking toward the posse. Breeze carried a small bag. Sonny Bee brushed something from the front of his clothes as he continued to come toward them.

"Let me talk to him first," said Jesse.

Breeze walked slightly behind Sonny Bee as they stopped in front of the posse. "What's happening?" asked Sonny Bee. He had a smile on his face.

Jesse wasn't smiling. "Everything. I just ruled you out. I'm taking over as posse leader."

Sonny Bee kept smiling. He placed his hands on his hips and looked at the ground before him. The end of his tongue seemed to part his lips as it moved back and forth. He lifted his head back to an upright position to look Jesse straight into his eyes. "Say what? Did I hear you right? Repeat that."

"You heard me right the first time, but I'm gonna say it again because I like the tone of that. I'm taking charge of the posse."

Sonny Bee stopped smiling. "You got a heck of a lot of balls. Who gave you the power to take my place and do any ruling." Sonny Bee looked at all the members. "You dudes down with him?"

All of them had a dumb look on their face. No one spoke.

"I elected myself. We tired of being used. All you want out of us is to do your dealing. You ain't nobody special. You ain't even on nobody's side. I saw that by the way you treated Scrap. If I hadn't bailed him out, he's still be in the Gray Bars Hotel."

"Hold it. Let me get you straight. These dudes know what's what around here."

"Yeah, I bet. We can sure see you ain't part of it. If that's what you're trying to tell us."

Sonny Bee raised his fist. He pointed his finger at Jesse. "You try to take over this territory and my posse, and you'll be barred away from here."

"You talk bad. Take away your ride and these drugs," he displayed a hand full, "and you're nothing. Jesse rolled his eyes in a dirty look and spat on the ground in front of Sonny Bee.

Sonny Bee jerked toward him. Somebody stepped out to grab him. He struggled to get lose. Another member had to jump in to help hold Sonny Bee back. A few seconds later, he stopped moving. The anger seemed to pass. A calm expression came to him. "Let me go. Everything's cool." They removed their hands. Sonny Bee straightened his clothes. "I'll tell you what I'll do. I'll give the posse the opportunity to choose who they want for a leader. All those who choose to be with Jesse, go stand next to him. Anyone willing to follow a real leader, come stand next to me." Sonny Bee backed off about ten feet so the group could separate themselves. Before anyone had a chance to move, six police cars pulled into the parking lot. The posse took notice.

"We'll do this later," said Jesse. "For now, let's beat it."

Everyone ran off in different directions. The officers climbed from their cars, took off running after them. Two were caught, while the others managed to get away. The two were brought back to the cars, searched, hand cuffed and put into one of the car's back seat. Two officers climbed into the front seat and the car was driven away. Several officers stayed and walked around the area.

All the Tenants had remained in their apartments until they thought the police had arrived and cleared the area of the drug dealers. Some came to their windows to look over the area below. Others started filtering onto the courtyard. A few ran to the officers standing around. This was a new day for the Tenants. From now on they were going to cooperate with the police in order to free themselves of the drug dealers and random crime which was getting farther out of control. They tried to explain what they saw during the time the action was in full swing. Some of the officers were glad to take notes. Some walked through the area showing concerns for the community. Children returned to play games they had started before everything broke out.

When the officers had established ground control, one of them called the Police Chief to inform him that they had successfully cleared the parking lot. This is when the Chief ordered half of the officers to spend the rest of the day there.

At a local television station, a news reporter sat at his desk hanging up the telephone from a local caller. He wrote a few words onto a note pad and pushed his chair away from his desk only to sit thinking for a moment. Suddenly, he jumped up from his seat and briskly walked to the Chief Editor's Office. He knocked twice before sticking his head inside unannounced.

"Why knock if you gonna just stick your head in. What can I do for you?"

The reporter walked in and took a seat directly in front of the editor's desk. He had the look of excitement about him. "I just finished talking with someone from the Miller Homes projects. They say there's a heck of a situation going on over there. They say the Tenants want someone from this office to come there to see if we can force the Police Chief and the Mayor to do something about things going on around there. They say we will be surprised and maybe print a story for other City Officials to read.

"I've been hearing rumors about things happening in that area."

"I think we should take the van, go over there and try to catch some of that action."

The Editor leaned back in his chair as far as it would go. He looked at the reporter. "Okay, you go there. I'll have a camera crew meet you. While you're there, try to talk to as many people as possible." He sat up straight close to his desk. "Get some real good scoop before you do any shooting. I know you got the news business in you."

The reporter shook his head in agreement and rushed from the office. On his way out of the building, he walked past his desk retrieving his note pad.

CHAPTER Thirteen

Bertha sat at the kitchen table across from her girlfriend. Empty plates laid in its center.

"I done got so I'm afraid to walk outside my door," said her girlfriend. "Living on the first floor isn't your Sunday go to meeting type of a situation. Every time those nuts in the courtyard and parking lot start acting up, I got to hide in fear of my life in my own apartment. It's terrible." She shook her head in anger.

"I'm glad I don't have the problem up here. All I got to do is pull my windows close to block out that mad world."

There was a moment of silence. Bertha hesitated to speak again. "I think you're right about that crack. I've been feeling sick lately when I can't get any. I don't like that feeling. I haven't been able to eat, not a drop. Look at me." She raised both arms and dropped them. "I don't weigh a lot in the first place. And now," she looked down at herself, "I done lost another twenty-two pounds. I'm gonna be as light as a pigeon soon."

Her girlfriend didn't look at all surprised. She raised a hand over her mouth trying to hold back a laugh. "I heard that. I know girl. You're starting to look bad. You got to give up that crack habit. I told you. You should have stuck with the weed."

"I know, you tried talking me out of using it. Like anybody else, sometimes I feel as though nobody can tell me anything. I realize you been right all the time. My kid stopped coming to visit me. He thinks I'm doing it up. And to make things worse, he said the money he was giving me, some of his friends said I was giving it to them for drugs. That hurt my feelings."

"I'll tell you, you got a smart kid."

"Yeah, I know. I didn't want him to know about me."

"How can he not know. We living I this warehouse community like sardines. Everybody knows everybody's business."

"That's the truth."

"Why don't you make him happy and turn yourself into a Rehabilitation Center. You can straighten yourself out and he wouldn't ever have to know."

Bertha looked surprised. She put her hand over her upper portion of her chest. "I can't do that. That's really putting myself out there. All that noise I made about drugs? Oh no, no way."

"Go to one out of town. Even better yet, out of state."

Bertha took her hand from her chest area and placed it on the table. "I don't know of any. Will you help me?"

"Hey." She reached across the table and patted the back of Bertha's hand. "That's what friends are for. But you know, when you do this, you can't go back to smoking marijuana, ever."

Bertha looked worried. "But I got to do something. Maybe things can go back to being like old time with you and me, you know."

"No, I'm afraid not. After seeing you go down like this, it scared me so that I gave up smoking weed. I got cheap. I couldn't afford the rolling papers."

Bertha laughed. "You pulling my leg, for real?"

"No child, I'm gonna take up cooking lessons." The both of them laughed together.

Bertha's boyfriend walked in through the front door. He came to the table to stand near Bertha's side. The two ladies laughed themselves out.

Bertha's girlfriend tightened her face to look up at him. "You got'ta stop supplying her with them drugs. Look at her." The room fell into a deep silence. "She wouldn't be like this if you'd learn to say no."

He became offended. "Hey, don't be jumping on me. She says she can't get enough. I got to work harder to keep both me and her going. In fact, she's been doing damn near all my own personal stash. So, you ain't just telling me something new. She won't listen to me."

"Well, I'm gonna help her. You can help too by keeping that stuff away from her. You do this for her and she'll love you more in the end."

Bertha had that look about her as if she wanted help. "Honey, she's gonna get me into a Rehab. Center so I can get myself straight. While I'm gone, you take care of the apartment."

"Baby, you done passed the point of no return. I gave you money to buy some grub. I ain't seen not one slice of bread around here. You telling me you gonna get straight? Case close." He walked to the front door and left.

The reporter pulled into the parking lot to find the police still there and a news crew sitting in a parked van. He walked to the van. The men inside were eating sandwiches and drinking sodas. "What do you guys think?" he asked.

"We can get out and set things up," said the driver between stuffing his mouth. "There just might be a story around here somewhere between these police and those Tenants." He wiped his mouth on the bare area of his arm.

The reporter gave the area a quick one hundred eighty-degree glance. "You guys finish eating while I take a look around." His voice was low. "I want to have a talk with a few Tenants. Maybe by then we can do a little shooting. This is some place."

"Help yourself," said the driver, while picking up a soda and drinking straight from the bottle. The rest of the men continued eating.

The reporter walked away toward the courtyard. The area turned out to be very orderly except for two men who was arguing with a police officer. Another man, who had seen the reporter near the van came to talk with him. They exchanged words. The reporter returned to the van. He looked excited. "Men, we got ourselves a story. Hand me the telephone. I'm gonna see if the Chief wants this on the air." The driver handed him a car phone. The reporter punched in a few buttons before placing it to the side of his face. His face glowed. "Yeah, get me the Editorial Chief." He looked around the area, his eyes came to rest on his crew. His finger shook as it pointed toward them. "Get the equipment ready." The words seemed to rush from between his lips. The crew started moving. The reporter spoke into the phone. Second later, when he had finished, he walked around to the back of the van. The crew had readied the equipment and now moving it toward the courtyard.

Some of the Tenants who saw the camera equipment began to move closer toward the crew.

"This spot will do fine," said the reporter. The crew began setting up.

"We'll be going on the air when the green light appears," said one of the technicians.

The reporter put on his hear gear and received a microphone from another member of the crew. He shook the wire to give himself more freedom of movement. A red light flashed on. "Thirty seconds to show time," shouted the driver.

The reporter watched a small timer next to the camera. Five, four, three, two, one, green. He looked straight into the camera. "We're standing in the courtyard of Miller Homes overlooking the area. It wouldn't be hard to see that there had indeed been some unusual activities taking place around here. The parking lot has several cars with bullet holes. From floor one through floor three of these high rise Towers, there are many shot out windows behind me as you can see. The lower part of the Towers looks as if someone has been chipping away at them, piece by piece. A Tenant who had previously spoke with me said things are getting worse day after day with no end in sight." Harry came to stand next to the reporter. The reporter took a quick glance toward him and returned his eyes to the camera. "He also told me that some of them have talked with the Mayor and representatives of the police force. Neither of them have responded in a way that the Tenants expected them to. I have a gentleman here who's been seeing things happening around here everyday." He turned toward the man. "Sir, how do you feel about the situation here?" He placed the microphone near Harry's chin.

"Terrible! I feel mad that this problem isn't getting any better. I feel bad that Tenants like me been living around here for years can't afford to move anywhere else. It's a darn shame when you get that feeling you gonna get robbed when you step out your apartment door. You see those apartments behind me." He turned for a split second to point toward the Towers. "I live back there. Picture yourself being in there when the sound of gun fire breaks out and you have to tell your family to get down on the floor at two o'clock in the afternoon to keep from getting killed. I don't know about anybody else, but I feel I'm living in a war zone. The Mayor's been promising and promising to make things better around here. We can't wait forever." He started shouting. "Do you hear me Mr. Mayor? Do something now."

The reporter pulled the microphone back toward his lips. "Well, you heard it first. And you seen it live. Thank you. This is YWZZP, Miller Homes.

That evening, the Police Chief held a meeting with his Operation Sweep Clean officers. "I've talked with the Mayor and the Judge," he said bluntly. "Between the two of them, I've yet to receive any satisfaction. I'm proposing to put a new plan into operation above our present one. It will require all of you for support. The only way to end this Miller Homes war is to force the drug dealers and thugs hand." The men's eyes followed him as he paced back and forth. "They have already shot one of my men, but not seriously." He stopped to face them. His expression was calm. "I've made arrangements with the surrounding Townships to house all the people we arrest in our next raid on Miller Homes. From what I've seen and heard so far, it looks like you might have a shoot out on your hands this time." He walked to his desk, took a seat. Anger over powered him. "I don't care if they are kids. If they shoot first." He vented his frustration with a thundering crash of his fist against the top of his desk. Several objects moved. A few officers jumped. "Shoot back. They're armed and dangerous. I want you, Officer Holt," looking into Holt's eyes, "take down my home phone number. Get it from my secretary. Call me right after you round them up. I need to know how many you have so I can tell you where to transport them. Are there any questions so far?"

Holt raised his hand.

"Speak Officer Holt."

"Chief, is this gonna be another one of though, catch'em let'em go deal?"

The Chief's eyes grew cold. A mysterious look about them set in. "No, we're going to lock them up this time. I want you men to hold this raid on Saturday morning when it's known that mostly all of them will be in the parking lot. Try not to get the Tenants involved. Wear your street clothes. I want all of you to approach the area at the same time, but from different angles. Much like you did the last time. There is one thing you have going against you. They know you guys are officers. So, proceed with caution. I hope this is going to be our last time dealing with these people. We got to make this one count. You got three days before we take action, be ready. If there aren't any further questions, we can end this meeting."

Bertha found out through her boyfriend that her son, Breeze had been arrested along with the other drug dealers in the operation. She called his father's house. Breeze was not there. She wanted so desperately to tell his father about what had happened, but being his father hadn't taken the time to keep up with his whereabouts, she let it go for fear of causing unnecessary pressure and harm to Breeze. She did leave word for him to call her as soon as he arrived.

That afternoon when Breeze returned home, he was given the message in a way which made it sound as if it was an emergency. He hurried to her apartment, running up the flights of steps tirelessly and down the hallway to her apartment. He tapped on the door until she opened it.

The sight of him brought tears to her eyes. He walked in with a worried look upon his face, waiting for her to say the first words.

She shut the door behind him. "Come here son. Let me hold you."

Puzzled, he came to her arms.

She hugged him and her tears wet his cheek.

"What's up Mom? Why all the tears?"

"I'm afraid for you," she managed to say.

He backed away from her. He looked even more puzzled. "Why should you be afraid for me? I'm old enough to take care of myself. You should know that." His face displayed a sign of relief. "You had me worried. Just think, I ran all the way over here thinking something had happened to you."

"Something did," she said. A tear rolled down her cheek. "I'm broken hearted. I have a feeling you might be going to jail."

"I ain't going…"

"Quiet son. I know all about you getting arrested with that parking lot gang. I should have stopped you long ago, but I didn't because of the money you was giving me. I can't let them take you away."

"Mom, don't scare me like this. Don't talk like that. I'm only fourteen. They don't put fourteen year olds in jail."

She placed her hands on both of his shoulders. "You don't know enough to understand what's going on in this world. I blame this whole situation on myself. I'm getting your things packed and having you sent down south where you can get away from this environment and your so-called friends. They don't mean you anything except harm. You need to be around kids who lead normal lives. This drug thing around here is no life for a kid. Listen to me because I mean what I say. It will make you worthless when you grow up. Your friends have no skills. Probably no education and nothing good going for them. You deserve better."

"But MOM! Those are my friends no matter what you say. They watch over me. We do things together."

Tears stopped flowing from her eyes. "I don't want you doing things with them. They do all the wrong things. Your life will be ruined." Suddenly, she began to smile as if a warm bright sun was shining down on her. "I would like to visit you in college. Not in jail. When you to get married. I would like for your family to be proud of you. To be a fine example for your children. A pillar in the community. And I too, will be proud of you."

He made no attempt to smile. "Aren't you proud of me now?"

"Yes, but I would feel even prouder if you were away from here."

He twisted her hands away from his shoulders while taking two steps backward. He looked annoyed. "Oh no! I don't wanna go down there."

"Son, listen. The situation around here has gotten so bad that grown folks are ready to kill all those in the parking lot selling drugs. If you're out there with them, they won't hesitate to hurt you as well."

Breeze thought for a moment. "Is it that bad around here?"

She shook her head, yes. "I'm going away myself for a couple of months."

His eyes brightened like his wish had come true. "Maybe we can go together." He started showing signs of excitement. "I know where we can go."

"No, my problem is different from yours. When I take care of what I have to take of, I'll come visit you."

Breeze was as happy as any teenager could be. "You promise?"

"Look, neither one of us can go living like we're living now. The bad things we do will one day come back to catch up with us."

"Okay then, but you'll have to promise to visit me."

"Sure, I promise." Her smile grew wide again. They gave each other a hug. "And you'll have to promise me you'll go," she said. "I can't tell you enough that it's for your own good."

"I promise," he replied.

They started walking toward the door. "Go home now. I'll call your father and tell him about you leaving. I'm not going to tell him why. He should have kept a closer eye on you." She showed signs of excitement. "I'll make arrangements for you to stay with your Aunt. She's been wanting you to come stay with her for the longest. She keeps telling me you'll love it there." Bertha let him out into the hallway and watch him until he disappeared through the stairway exit.

The crack she had smoked earlier during the day was still taking an effect on her, but she knew she had to take care of these matters for herself and for her son who she loved dearly.

The sun disappeared from the sky a short time ago. Darkness covered the streets except in areas where street lights and store lights were visible. Flash leaned against a large store front glass. The upper portion of his body cast a long leading silhouette against the sidewalk. He was possessed with anger. It wasn't often that someone had made him look like a punk in front of his posse. This was the first time since he was twelve that he had been caught red handed in this type of situation without a weapon. All he thought about was how to get even with the undercover officer. He didn't care about Sonny Bee's posse or even Sonny Bee. He knew where he could find them anytime. But this officer knew things about him and wasn't afraid to make his stand. Flash knew he would never again go without his pistol. It was dumb of him not to have taken it with him in the first place.

Maybe if he went back to Miller Homes, he might be able to stir up some action.

Miller Homes was only two blocks away. Lifting himself from the glass, he started walking. There was a field just behind his Aunt's high rise. He breathed heavily in the night air as he hastily followed a walk path leading to the back stairway. Several times he balled his fist and punched his other hand as he mumbled along the way.

He reached an open doorway. It was fairly dark inside. He began to climb upward. At times he would feel for the railing. He stepped on something soft, it made a cat noise. He stopped, grabbed his heart. "Damn, I think I got a load in my pants." A cat ran down the steps. Flash laughed. "That'll teach you not to get in my way." He continued on his way until reaching the floor where she lived. He walked down the hall and knocked on her door. From where he stood, he could see movement within the little peep hole in the center on the door. He moved closer for a better look. Before he could get his sight into place, the door opened part way. His Aunt stood staring at him. He blinked a couple of times in surprise.

"I should of known it wouldn't be anyone other than that boy," she said, her face showing signs of disappointment. "You the only person I know who would have enough nerve to come around here at night."

She opened the door wider. "Get in here before those thugs start running up and down this hallway. Things happen to people in these halls at night. I'd hate to see something happen to you. I just might have a heart attack."

He walked into the kitchen, looking around as he took a seat at the table.

She started cleaning around the stove.

"Auntie, why don't you call out for pizza?" he said out of the clear blue.

She kept on working, trying to remove a hard spot. "Lordy be," she said. "When brains were passed out, you must have stepped out of line." She stopped for a moment, stared at him, and went back to cleaning. "I done told you over and over, time after time I don't like no pizza. I can't stand the cheese."

"It ain't for you. I can handle it."

"Why didn't you get one before you came here?" She stopped to ball up her cleaning rag. "I know, you think people got money all the time, like it grows on trees. Is that what you came over here for? A pizza?"

"Not really, the pizza was something my stomach asked for." He gave her a gentle smile. "What I really need is a place to spend the night. I'm so tired, I can't even walk home."

She placed some pots into the sink and turned back to face him. "I don't understand you at all. You walked here." She pointed to the floor. "Here, to tell me you can't walk home?"

"No, you got that wrong. I was closer to here than home, so I came by to see my favorite Auntie. You know I think a lot of you. When I die and if you should still be around, I'm gonna leave you all my worldly wealth."

She couldn't help but to break down and laugh. "You know, you are crazier than I thought. Listen, listen closely. When you die, do me a favor, take everything you got with you. It would cost me more to keep that mess then to have it buried with your body."

Now it was his turn to laugh. "I told Mom you had a sense of humor. Maybe I could stay here and be your bodyguard."

"Oh no," she was quick to respond, holding her hands up as if a gun was sticking in her back. "I'd feel safer staying by myself. Its been that way for years."

"Okay, if you want it that way. I hope you know there's some tough dudes out there. I know what they're all about. I ain't afraid of none of them."

"I know you ain't." She went back to cleaning.

He rose from his chair, and walked to the front window. The view fascinated him. He gently moved a section of curtains to one side and began staring down onto the courtyard. He leaned forward, putting his hands around the sides of his face. "Just the person I been wanting to see," excitingly, he said.

"I hadn't given the pizza another thought." Her soft voice spilled out into the front room. "Sometimes I wonder if your mother had any kids that lived."

By now he was out the door and on his way to the steps. "I heard that," he called back in a fading voice. "And I'm not brain dead if that's what you mean."

She shook her head from side to side as she went to close the front door.

Flash rushed down the steps and across the courtyard trying to catch up with Jesse. Jesse heard the rapid footsteps coming his way. He turned to see Flash charging toward him. In an act of self defense, Jesse pulled his pistol, quickly raising it with his trigger finger readied. At the moment Flash saw the pistol, he stopped dead in his tracks, almost falling forward. At the same time, he put his hands high in the air. People sitting on benches rose to their feet and started running into the nearest high rise with the thought of more violence breaking out.

"Don't shoot," he screamed, showing signs of being winded.

"I ought to fill you full of holes for the way you been making trouble around here. What you want?"

Flash started walking closer.

"I think you've gotten close enough. Take one more step and you're history."

Flash stopped advancing. A smile began to appear on his face. "I think its about time our two posse's got together and became one. I heard Sonny Bee's boys left him for you."

"That ain't none of your business. Who told you that?"

Flash started lowering his arms. Jesse extended his pistol's reach to point straight at Flash's chest. Flash jerked his arms up again. "I think we ought to have a little rap session," said Flash. "Just you and me. I know what's going on around here. I ain't as dumb as everybody think I am. You should know me by now after all these years, I don't miss a thing."

"We don't need to rap. I ain't got nothing to say to you. I got my own thing, you dig! I can make it without you. Put your hands down before somebody calls the Knights on us. But the warning still goes." Jesse lowered the pistol below his waist line with caution.

"Someday you gonna need my help. Just you wait and see. Think about what I said."

"What with you man? One day you and your gang's ripping us off. Days later, you want to join up with us."

"I'll tell you what. I'll give you back all the drugs we took from you plus enough to make up for the cash. That should square that. And we won't pull anymore raids around here, that's if your posse backs off with their attempt to get even."

"I can't promise you anything, but I'll rap to them. They lost a lot of face because of the stupid raid you pulled."

"Look," said Flash, showing signs of frustration, "I said I'll keep my posse down. What you want, blood?"

"Why did you waste Butch?"

Flash threw his hands up and down in a flurry of motions. Jesse raised his pistol, ready to shoot at any second. Flash grew scared.

"Don't play that hand stuff with me," Jesse said as a warning. "Keep 'em still before I feed you a six pack." Jesse lowered the pistol again.

Flash began to breathe a little easier. "All, man, lets not get into that. I ain't here to hurt you. And that Butch thing really wasn't nothing."

"I want to hear about it anyway."

"You know the dude was a punk. He was easy game. I just went off on him when I saw his pistol pointed at me. If I hadn't got him, my posse would have turned against me."

"So you blew him away?"

"Hey, I had to save face. Besides, he threatened me. Word got around that he had a gun. I wasn't ready for the pie in the sky. So, what about it, can we hook up?"

"I don't know why I'm saying this, but I'll give it a thought when I'm not busy. For now, get out of my sight before I forget I got a heart and do the rest of the world a favor. The next time I see you, I might not be this soft."

Flash raised his hands as if to surrender, and ran back into the high rise.

"He almost scared the daylight out of me," said Jesse, in a low voice as he turned to walk away.

Jesse made his way up to Sonny Bee's apartment. Sonny Bee let him in and took the dog into his bedroom. Seconds later, he came out to lock the dog inside. When he returned to the front room, Jesse was sitting on the sofa.

"What you come up here for?" asked Sonny Bee, his tone of voice was rough.

"I didn't come up here to cop no plea, if that's what you're expecting. We need to rap."

"About what? You got the posse under your command."

"Yeah, I know, but that's minor compared to what we need to rap on. I could have been any dude. They looking for real leadership if you can dig where I'm coming from."

Sonny Bee flared up in anger. "You telling me I ain't no leader?"

Jesse remained calm. "To be honest, no. You're still a good dude, but check this out. The posse is getting older in age. They started to fall under pressure from other posses. They need somebody right there at times to give them strength and support to fight off other dudes. Right now, face it. You got other things you want to take care of. You ain't got time for them. The only time we see each other, and that includes the posse, is when you need to collect some money or pass off."

Sonny Bee pointed a stiff finger toward Jesse. "Let me tell you something. It seems hard for you to understand what this business is all about. What you dudes doing out there ain't real business. Anybody can stand out there and hustle a few nickel and dimes. I ain't got time for all that stuff. You're right, I'm dealing with real people who make you possible."

Jesse jumped up from the sofa steaming mad. He pointed a finger back toward Sonny Bee. "Hold it right there! Sonny Bee you know." He squinted his eyes. "You got some grapes in saying that. Anytime we standing out there, that's business. Let me tell you something else."

Sonny Bee started showing signs of anger as well. "Tell me man! Tell me! All of a sudden you got a brain storm." Sonny Bee's body grew tense.

Jesse turned a finger toward himself. "I quit school when I was fourteen. I figured the teachers couldn't teach me anything I didn't already learn from the streets." He lunged his finger against his chest several times. "I make myself possible, not you. This is a tough world. You make it fast or anyway you can. We living for today. Tomorrow's not promised to any of us. So we ain't into that sophisticated stuff. Them nickels and dimes add up. We making more cash than those dudes with the white shirts and ties, all dolled up. We gonna live right. The heck with you if that didn't register."

Sonny Bee relaxed himself. "All you dudes got your heads screwed on backward. You should be hustling and saving. Look at what I got. A car, an apartment, money saved and any broad I want."

"If that's the way you think, you working with the wrong dudes. That's why they need a new leader. I'm the oldest now. I know the posse's too young for some of those things. Maybe if you had been out there with them, giving them a dream, they might be moving in a better direction as you put it."

"With all the doe they done made by now, I would of thought they had gotten their priorities straight."

"Here we go again." Jesse walked to the window and back shaking his head. "Priorities! Yeah, they got them. Those dudes said they ain't never gonna work for anybody that's gonna pay less then what they making a day selling drugs. Minimum wage, just ain't, gonna, get, it. That's out! Would you work for minimum wages?"

There was a knock at the door. Sonny Bee went to open it. It was Breeze. Sonny Bee walked away leaving the door open. Breeze walked in surprised to see Jesse. Breeze didn't speak to him, just gave a mean look. "I guess you know the whole posse went over to Jesse's side," Breeze said, staring into Jesse's eyes. "I didn't. I'm with you for as long as I'm still here."

Sonny Bee gave Breeze a surprise look. Jesse looked down at the floor, scratched the back of his neck. Then started walking toward the front door. Sonny Bee and Breeze had their eyes focused on him.

"See you around, Sonny Bee," Jesse said as he went out the door, closing it behind him.

Sonny Bee turned his focus to Breeze. "What you mean for as long as you're here? You planning on making a move?"

Breeze walked to the other side of the room. He stared out the window. "My Momma said it was about time I moved on. She's sending me away, down south."

Sonny Bee exploded. "Damn, I ain't got nobody."

"Yes you do," Breeze replied, turning sideways to face Sonny Bee. "You got Sandy. She's like your private aide."

"I said, I ain't got nobody." He threw his hands in the air. "That's okay. I'll start another posse in another area."

"I'm sorry things went down the way they did for you. My Mom said, I got to live a better life than what I'm living now."

Sonny Bee ignored Breeze by talking to himself. "I'll build a new empire. Live high on it." He made a fist. "Yeah, that's just what I'll do,"

Breeze noticed a certain glow in his eyes. Sensing something wasn't right, he slowly walked toward the door.

Sonny Bee kept talking. He seemed all charged up. "Get some broads working. Maybe get Sandy back to doing her thing with the dog."

Breeze eased his way out into the hallway and slowly closed the door behind him.

CHAPTER Fourteen

The next morning, Flash awakened around 10 a.m. His Aunt had earlier left for work. The apartment was quiet. He eased from the bed and made his way to the refrigerator. He opened the door as wide as it would open. Everything seemed blurred inside. He wiped his eyes with the back of his hand before extending his arms over his head to stretch. He twisted them in the air, and bent forward to pick through the objects inside.

He took out a quart of milk and a small tray of butter. Placing them on a nearby counter. He grabbed two slices of bread from a nearby open loaf, placing them into the toaster. He pushed the lever down. Watched for a moment until a red glow appeared. With this part taken care of, he walked off to the bathroom to wash up. After he had finished, he stared into the mirror. "You handsome devil," he said to himself with admiration. Then left for the bedroom to put on his clothes. By the time he started buttoning his shirt, the smell of burnt toast sent him running into the kitchen. Upon seeing flames, he rushed to the toaster. Picked it up. Placed it into the sink. A short electrical cord jumped toward him. He thinned out the smoke pouring from the toaster by rapidly fanning his hands back and forth. A small glowing flame inside died out. The end of a slice of bread had gotten stuck in the slide, preventing the toaster from shutting off. He stared down at the slices. All that remained was two pieces of chard substances. "Damn, can't do anything right," he said disgustingly. Breakfast was shot. He left the sink and walked out the door. He has so much on his mind that he walked away leaving the door wide open. A little ways down the hall he thought about the door. It was no big thing to him. Many times before he had forgotten to close it. Maybe that's why his Aunt didn't want him staying there.

When Flash reached the courtyard, the sun was already shining brightly. He was forced to squint his eyes to fight off the sun glare. The temperature was already up and he was starting to feel the heat while waiting for his eyes to get adjusted to the light. "What a way to start the day," he mumbled before taking a deep breath of city air. Slowly he let it out before walking toward the parking lot.

The lady whom he had stolen the pocketbook from ran up behind him. She started hitting the back of his head and shoulders with an old black pocketbook she held. "You good for nothing," she screamed. "Where's my pocketbook and all my things that was inside?"

In shock, he turned, trying to shield himself from her awkward blows with one hand while trying to reach for his concealed pistol with the other. Finally, he was able to retrieve it and quickly raised it to point at her. Upon seeing the weapon, she fainted. Flash walked away, straightening his clothes and returning the pistol to his waist band. The lady continued to lay still on the concrete path. The few Tenants who witnessed the incident thought it to be the funniest thing. They laughed instead of going to her aide.

Flash walked up behind Jesse, who was standing in the parking lot. When Jesse took notice, he spun around, placing his hand against the butt of his pistol under his shirt. "Don't ever do that again," he said angrily. "I don't trust you and neither does anyone else. I thought I told you to keep your distance?"

"I just wanted to know if you thought over what we talked about last night?"

"I told you I'd think about it. Give me a few more days. You really serious about this?"

"Yeah. I'm trying to change my image."

Jesse laughed with one hand over his mouth. "I doubt if we can help you. You got a long ways to go."

"I know," said Flash as if to be making a confessing gesture.

Jesse became uneasy. "Where's the stuff you claimed you could cop?"

Flash became angry. "We only talked last night. Give me a chance."

Jesse stared down at him. Flash took that as a sign of mistrust and walked away.

Bertha's girlfriend and boyfriend were sitting at the kitchen table smoking while Bertha cooked something for all of them to eat.

"I talked with this guy on the telephone yesterday," said her girlfriend. "He told me that if you was willing to check in within the next twelve hours, they would save a bed for you." She took a joint from Bertha's boyfriend. Took a long drag and passed it back to him.

"I thought you quit smoking weed'" said Bertha.

"I only quit for a little while. My nerves done went bad on me listening to all that noise outside."

Bertha carried some food to the table. "I sure hope you don't expect me to go today, do you?"

"I would think the sooner you go, the better off you'll be."

"Oh no. It won't be for a couple of days yet. I just made some phone calls. Breeze will be leaving town between this evening and tomorrow morning. Hopefully, this evening. His father said he would pack his stuff. He's going south you know, to be with family. I don't mean the south side of town. I mean the real place like behind the cotton curtain." She went back to get herself a plate. She returned with it and a quart of juice, seated herself and began to fill her plate. She glanced across the table.

"Honey, I'm gonna need fifty dollars for cigarettes and other things while I'm gone."

He took fifty dollars from his wallet and passed it across the table to her. "Don't spend it all in one place," winking his eye.

She smiled.

Her girlfriend looked up from her plate. "Well, if you don't go today, I'll have to call them back. Are you sure you'll be ready in a couple of days?"

"I should be. I want to make sure Breeze gets off first. I need to get my welfare check on Mother's Day so I can pay my rent plus some other small bills I owe. Them people," she said disgustingly, "keep writing and threatening to come take this little bit of stuff back if I don't make another payment. They got some nerve. It's a shame the way them folks waste money and squeeze us poor people of every penny. I guess that's all part of the business."

"I hope Tuesday will be a good day for you. You should be looking and feeling great when you return. This place will do wonders for you if you follow their program."

"I'll do the best I can."

"I'll come over here now and then to make sure he keeps this place clean while you're gone."

Bertha placed a spoon filled with food in front of her mouth as if to be talking to it. She looked straight toward her boyfriend. "Honey, tell me you're happy for me."

He looked up from his plate. "Baby, you know I am. I'm so happy that you're getting yourself together. We can start saving for that dream house."

She pushed his shoulder. They smiled pleasantly at each other. They started eating from the plate in front of them.

That evening, the television reporter sat behind his desk working on some notes he had collected from a conversation with the Mayor and Police Chief. They had provided very little information, but with the aide from various newspaper clippings, he was able to get a picture of why the officials had been dragging their feet in ridding Miller Homes of its trouble makers. The conclusion seemed hard to digest, but they appeared to be true. He red silently over his writing, realizing it was a black community. Most of the Tenants were on welfare or some form of government assistance and most likely making no contribution toward society. Most of the town's drug activity was centered in this one area away from the working class. The city officials felt the issue of drugs was secondary or beyond in non-white neighborhoods. *This is a terrible way to judge a small community where people are supposed to be created equally under the American way of life. Why use the measurement of a selected few to judge the whole. It can't continue like this.* He decided to do more writing, give it to the Editorial Chief for possible airing. Maybe this would spark quicker action, which is the most needed thing at this moment.

The following morning, Breeze was standing on his father's door step when Bertha, riding in a yellow cab pulled up to the curb. Sitting in the rear seat, she leaned forward and said a few words to the driver. He got out, opened the trunk section and walked up to Breeze. Breeze had a far away look in his eyes. The driver took both suitcases and placed them inside the trunk. He walked around to the side of the cab facing Breeze, bent slightly as he pulled the door open. Breeze could see his mother sitting uneasy in the seat. "Come son," she called while waving to him at the same time.

Breeze walked to the cab, climber inside without speaking. The driver returned to the drive's seat. Meanwhile, Breeze rolled down the window and began staring at his father's house. Second later, the cab pulled away to merge into a stream of traffic.

The day had finally arrived. It was Saturday morning. Six officers, who had been instructed by the Chief to rid Miller Homes of the drug dealers assembled at the police station to pick up their cars. They synchronized their watches. At 11:30 a.m., their plan called for them to walk out from behind Miller Homes building, do whatever was necessary and that would be the end of that.

They climbed into two unmarked cars. The cars rolled passed their designated area. Holt, who was seated in the first car, checked to make sure the dealers were in the parking lot. Two blocks beyond Miller Homes, the cars were parked. All six men got out. They walked back one block, passing two patrol wagons at their assigned station. Before splitting up into two groups of threes, Holt told them he wanted them to spread out. One group would come in from the right side while the other group would come in from the left rear.

Almost at mid point of the last block, the groups drifted apart while continuing toward their objective. Holt looked at his watch. *Five minutes to show time* he thought. He and his two fellow officers reached their side of Miller Homes. They were stationed on a blind side to the parking lot, out of sight. The three men checked their pistols and returned them to their holster. Holt's two fellow officers removed their sun glasses, neatly folding them before placing them into their pocket. Holt checked his watch again. The other three should have been in position by now. It was now 11:30 a.m. As the three moved from around the corner's edge, they observed the other three stepping out in their approach toward the dealers. Both groups started spreading out as they continued to move forward. One of the dealers spotted them. "Hey guys, looks like we got company," he shouted.

"We ain't gonna run from them this time," Jesse called out. "Lets take cover."

People buying drugs didn't know what was about to take place. Dealers took to moving behind cars. Buyers followed asking questions and still trying to make deals.

Holt, looking to see that his men had positioned themselves for good all around cover, started the ball rolling. He pulled out his pistol. The other five did the same.

"This is a bust." he shouted at the top of his lungs. Buyers started running away from the parking lot. Three cars on the roadway raced away. The parking lot looked like a three ring circus.

"Everyone remain still," came the next command. Dealers moved even quicker now, getting behind parked cars. Buyers got cold feet. They stopped in their tracks. Jesse hollered out from behind a parked car, "Blast them."

The posse opened fire on the officers. Buyers dove for the ground. The officers returned fire while retreating to the building's edges. One officer from the left side was struck down. He laid motionless next to a Tower in the dirt. Dealers became pinned down to a point which prevented them from relocating, but had good firing positions between cars. Another officer from Holt's group dodged forward toward a dumpster to get a better position, was hit. His body jerked forward as he fell face down five feet from his goal. By now, no one was left standing in the surrounding areas. They had either ran for cover or was laying flat against the ground's surface. This included people in the courtyard.

The exchange of gun fire grew intense. One of Jesse's boys stood up to get off a better shot. Alone bullet struck his chest. He went flying backward as if being jerked by a rope. Another had his pistol shot from his hand. He grabbed his wrist in a wild scream of pain. Two more officers started advancing. One from both ends. One from the right made it safety to a barren tree. The other managed to get close to a parked car.

Flash and eight of his posse members appearing in the distance observed what was taking place. Flash led his advancing men up behind the remaining four officers. This left the officers between Jesse's posse in front and Flash's posse in the rear. The officers took notice of Flash's posse. Thinking of them as just a bunch of kids watching, they thought nothing of them coming closer.

Jesse smiled when he saw Flash.

Flash's posse opened fire.

Jesse knew the officers were caught in a cross fire. He and his posse began to pour out more shots.

Holt and his two fellow officers were now in trouble. Holt's partner was shot in the back. Holt turned to face flash's posse. A hail of bullets struck him. He flurried to the ground and laid motionless with his eyes wide open. The last two officers dropped at the same time.

Jesse's posse sensing it was all clear stopped firing. The group took off running toward the high rise apartments.

Buyers laying on the ground, seeing the dealers running away came to their feet and they also ran off as well.

Flash and his posse moved in closer to take a look at the bodies and faces. Some of them had to be rolled over. Flash looked at each face hoping to find the officer who pulled the gun on him. "Damn," he said. "You got away this time, we even. Score, one for you, one for me."

At 2:00 p.m., the District Police Chief called the police station. He was informed that there had been another shootout around Miller Homes. Seven black males had been killed. They had no identification on them. A special crew of medical people would have to be called in to identify the bodies. The Chief hung up the telephone, briskly walked out of the building to his car and drove away in a hurry to the city morgue.

The Chief requested to see the bodies. An attendant led him away to a large room on the lower level. They entered the room to find six bodies stretched out in a single row along the floor covered with sheets. The Chief walked around lifting each sheet to see their faces. When he had seen the last face, he held his head down. "These are my men," he said in a low voice. "Something had to seriously go wrong for them not to be able to handle a bunch of young drug dealers." He became silent momentarily. "If anyone wants me, I'll be either in my office or at home." He walked to the door's entrance, pushed his way through and disappeared.

Bertha's boyfriend had gotten shot in the shoulder during the battle with the officers. He didn't realize it until he ran into the building when one of his posse members noticed the blood on his shirt sleeve. "Hey Bro., you get hit or something? Better go check it out." The only safe place he could possibly go now without getting picked up by the police would be to Bertha's apartment.

The gang member left, dashing back onto the courtyard. Bertha's boyfriend began to take a closer look at the blood stained area. It didn't feel as bad as it looked. He would have her take a look at it and maybe give him some advice. He walked to the edge of the first step and looked straight up trough the narrow opening. It looked far up. He had to think twice before making any move.

"This is a heck of a time to be climbing five flights of steps." He said still confused. The feeling of blood dripping from his finger tips into a puddle forming near his feet told him to go up. He tried touching the wound but as pain started to set in, he let it go. With blood dripping the way it did, he chose to make the climb.

Step after step after step, upward he went. Good hand on the railing. Bad arm hanging limp like. The trip wasn't like going to the corner store. It took a lot more energy then effort. At one point, he stopped to look behind him. A close trail of blood spots continued to follow him as far as he could see. He couldn't help for thinking about his shoulder wound. He stared at it. His eyes followed a wet red line running down the length of his arm. The blood seemed to be oozing faster than before. He pressed his good hand over the wound. Instantly, the touch created pain which caused his facial expression to go sour. He immediately took his hand away. A sudden urge gave him the impulse to continue onward.

He tried to pace himself but around midway he tired. The urge to go on died. He eased into a sitting position on the hard concrete steps and looked down at the puddle forming next to him. Fear of possibly dying sparked him into trying again. "Of all times," he said in a low voice. "Not one person walking on these steps. Any other time of the day, somebody would be running me over." He regained his standing position and continued on his way.

Upon reaching her floor, he began to feel weak from the lost of blood. It had been a long journey upward. He leaned against the wall, dropping into a sitting position on the hallway floor. The bullet was causing much pain now. He began tearing away the blood soaked sleeve to expose the wounded area. The tearing process caused more pain than he expected. In a last effort, he gave the cloth a hard pull. Blood started flowing faster. He cried out in pain. His hand released the sleeve. "The hell with this," he cried out. Someway he had to get the bleeding to stop or he'd surely bleed to death. Out of anger, he managed to tear a portion of the sleeve lose, but the part nearest the top wouldn't give way. The pain became so intense, he gave up. He moved away from the wall to lay flat on the floor.

Everything in the hallway began to rotate. Thoughts began to dance across his mind. First, there was Flash. *Why did he come to help? Is he that much of a savage to want to kill just for the sake of killing? It was good he showed up when he did. It might have been me laying out there. But how do I go about trusting him. I better talk with Jesse. He seems to be the only dude who can get along with him.*

And there was Bertha. Do she really have to go away? I could cut off her supply of drugs. After a couple weeks, she would be okay again, or was she trying to find away to get away from me.

I've been treating her good every since she flipped out over Butch. Maybe I can rap to her. Get her to understand that I'll be lonely without her. Let me stop dreaming. I got to get to that apartment before I bleed to death."

He managed to pull himself up into a sitting position. The pain was still there but he knew he needed help in the worse way. Now was not the time to be sitting around. He leaned over far enough to get his good hand against the floor. Then managed to get into a kneeling position. His hand and knees were starting to get covered with blood that had accumulated near him. He sturdy himself in this position, took a deep breath and lifted his body straight up. Once on his feet, he became dizzy and almost fell backward.

He made his way to the apartment. At the door he stopped. "Bertha." Softly the word came from between his lips. He waited. No response. With the open palm of his hand, he slapped the door once hard and then again slightly softer while passing out and sliding to the floor into a semi-ball.

The reporter heard about the shoot out on Miller Homes ground. He and his crew rushed to the area to find the last police car pulling away. The bodies had already been removed. People gathered in groups around the courtyard discussing what they saw and though. The reporter walked around trying to gather any information that might be worth reporting. People, who were so eager to talk with him before, now either talked low or clamped up when he approached them. He tried asking questions but received very little information. He began to realize that the Tenants didn't want to be exposed on national television as part of what had happened in fear of possible repercussions.

Later that evening, the Police Chief sat behind his desk looking down at today's newspaper. It amazed him how fast the press was able to come up with enough news for printing. The headlines read: SHOOTOUT AT MILLER HOMES LEAVES SEVEN MALES DEAD. He flipped the newspaper over. Still he couldn't help but to wonder how his men had managed to let those young drug dealers get the drop on them. There had to be a way of apprehending those kids without injuring Tenants, but how, was a mystery. He knew most of his officers in this area were not capable of doing what he wanted done in a fashion he desired. These officers were mostly white males and would stick out like sore thumbs.

The Chief would never admit to defeat. It dawned on him, the only thing left for him to do would be to seek advice from another source. The State Police Colonel was a powerful and smart man. He would have a suggestion or two if asked the right question. The Chief picked up the telephone, dialed several numbers. He waited a few seconds for a response. "Colonel, this is the Police Chief." Silence. "I'm sorry that I'm just getting to speak with you about a big problem I'm having. I need some advice on how to capture a bunch of kids." Silence. "Sure, I'll come over right away. Let's see what we can come up with."

Bertha's boyfriend lay in bed asleep with a cold towel across his forehead. Bertha had removed most of his clothing and shoes. One of his shoulders was bandaged with a small red spot over the center of the wound. He stirred, then squinted his eyes. The slight movement caused him to moan, creating a sudden pain in his shoulder. This awakened him.

Outside the room, he could hear Bertha talking with someone. "Bertha," he called out in a weak voice.

She walked through the opened doorway to his bedside. "You sure looked a mess when I came home and found outside my door. I was horrified with the thought that you were dead. After checking your vital signs, I found you still breathing. You were too heavy to carry, so I dragged you in here and cleaned you up. What happened to you?"

"Those undercover dudes came back to try to take us in. Jesse schooled us that we had a better chance at going down with it than to be taken in. It was my dump luck to get shot."

"You must be in big trouble by now. I heard all six of police officers were killed. It's on the news and everything."

"If that's so, I wouldn't know. I left them there."

"From the look of that wound, it looks like you still have a bullet in you. I need to get you help." She made an attempt to leave the room. He was quick to respond.

"No!" he responded as loud as his voice could be raised. She stopped on his command. He was staring at her when she turned to face him. "That's what they're waiting for. Someone to show up at a hospital with bullet wounds."

"I know this doctor," she said. "Maybe I can convince him to come take it out secretly."

"That sounds good. Give him a try, but make sure you get him to keep it a secret. I don't want to see an army of Knights staring down at me and asking dumb questions, that's if they don't shoot first." She walked out of the room. Seconds later, he heard her talking again. The apartment door opened and closed. There was silence.

"Bertha," he called out once again. No one answered. He closed his eyes.

CHAPTER Fifteen

The Police Chief restored the security to Miller Homes. He assigned a total of six new officers around the area. Two in the parking lot, two in the courtyard and the remaining two in the housing area. They were instructed to patrol these areas only during day light hours. This left the dealers to operate under the cover of darkness. Some of the Tenants began to feel pleased that someone downtown had finally taken a stand on their side. Some felt safe to roam throughout the area during the day and let their children play freely. Others were uncertain about this security because of what had happened to the other officers.

Days later, a member of Jesse's posse stood by a bench in the courtyard reading the front page of the newspaper to most of the posse who had gathered around him. "It says that an ongoing investigation is underway into the deaths of six officers shot in the back. They were killed in Miller Homes Projects." A smile came on his face as he looked up. "Jesse, we cleared from this mess. We were shooting from the front."

"Trigger happy Flash gonna burn for sure on this one," said Jesse.

The kid turned the page. He pulled the paper close to his face. "Hey! Check this out." All eyed turned toward him. "Here's a special announcement added in: CONVENTION HALL OPENS ITS DOOR TO FREE CITY CONCERT. I like it. I like it."

Everyone began to agree.

"What's it says?" Jesse asked.

"It says," 'The concert is given in an effort to provide some form of entertainment for all school age kids from ten to eighteen years of age. One hundred prizes will be given to lucky ticket holders. Prizes ranging from paid trips to televisions to bikes. The show will be star studded with exciting entertainment.' "I don't know about you dudes, but I'm gonna check it out."

"I'm down with it too," said one of the members. "When is it going down?"

He red in silence. "Hey man," he responded in a joyous outburst, "This coming Wednesday, starting at 6 p.m.

"Great. All those kids. I'm loading up. There's gonna be a ton of dudes there. I could probably unload my whole stash before the show starts. And if I win something," the kid exploded with excitement. "Man, that would be an out of sight night."

Jesse wasn't too thrilled about the show. His thoughts were somewhere else. "Did anybody talk to the dude who got shot in the shoulder?"

"Yeah, I did," answered a tall lanky kid about sixteen years old. "He didn't look like he got hurt too bad. Think he went up to his old lady's crib. I left him standing inside the building."

The kid who was reading the paper stared at Jesse. "Why you change the subject? I was on a roll with this exciting news. This kind of stuff is good for the pocket and the head."

"Ditch the news," said Jesse. "Let blow this area and get some grub. My stomach tells me its time to do it." Jesse became motionless. "Better yet, you dudes go ahead. I got to take care of some business I almost forgot about."

The posse walked out of the courtyard, leaving Jesse standing in the same spot.

The officer in the courtyard walked out of sight.

Jesse went to Flash's Aunt apartment hoping to find him there. He thought it was about time the two had a talk. On arrival, Jesse tapped on the door.

Flash opened it wide. He stuck his chest out. It was his way of showing people how tough he was. "Come on in. So you ready to talk?" Jesse opened his mouth to speak, but Flash was quick with more words to express his point. "I knew you would be needing me sooner or later." Jesse walked in. "Have a sit down on the sofa. My Aunt ain't here right now, so no problem out of her. She's the only person I know who's tougher than me."

Jesse squinted his eyes as he took notice of the crazy look looming on Flash's face. "How did you know those undercover dudes were out to nail us?"

Flash looked surprised. "I didn't. Me and my posse was coming down to see if we could make some cash floating around in the lot. Seeing what was going down, me and my posse figured this was our shot to let you know we wanted in."

"So you want to join up with us that bad?"

"Yeah, together our posse would have a stronger hold on Miller Homes territory."

"After that heroic deed you and your posse displayed, I'm gonna let you dudes in. But there's one condition."

"What's that?" frowned Flash. "I hope it ain't something stupid."

"I'm in charge, you dig. I run the activities and no dumb stuff out of you. All that crazy stuff you been doing is in the past." He sliced the air between them with the side of his hand, "Is zeroed out. You got that?"

Flash looked relieved. "That's no problem. Your good at holding the cards."

"I think we should rap to our posse and let them know about the merger." Flash looked up toward the ceiling. "Yeah, were getting stronger and bad. I feel like we can take on the whole world."

Jesse eased back on the sofa to rest his back. He was not happy with Flash's last remark. "That's the kind of dumb stuff I was just talking about. I wouldn't push my luck that far if I was you."

"Dig Jesse, that was just talk. You know how easy I get excited."

The sound of locks turning caused them to stop talking. The apartment became quiet. The knob turned completely and the door opened. Auntie stepped in. She stopped upon seeing Jesse.

Flash jumped to his feet. His mouth opened but no words came out.

She pointed toward Jesse. "You one of those dealers from out in the parking lot." Before Jesse could utter a word, she began to blast him. "Get out of here right this minute." Jesse rose, not saying a word, walked pass her and out into the hallway.

She stared at Flash with angered eyes. "The next time I see one of those things in here," she slammed the door close, "I'm gonna throw you out with him. You hear that?"

Flash gave in to her demand. "Yeah, Auntie. We were only talking."

"The next time he'll be taking things out of here."

"You don't trust anybody do you?"

"Why should I. Maybe you don't know where you're at." She walked off toward her bedroom.

Flash started babbling as he walked out the front door.

Bertha managed to convince the doctor to come to her apartment. He extracted the bullet from her boyfriend's shoulder. Her boyfriend lay asleep while the doctor returned his medical tools to its bag.

"He's going to need plenty of rest," said the Doctor. "It's good you stopped the bleeding when you did. He was almost a goner. The bullet chipped a piece of bone in his shoulder. If he doesn't get it taken care of soon, he'll probably develop some limited use of that arm. Here's a prescription, make sure he takes it." He took a pad from his bag, wrote something on it. Tore away the top sheet, handed to her.

"I want to thank you," she said, "I'll make sure he takes this."

"He should be alright for now. If anything develops, and you want me to talk with him, give me a call. Here's my card." He pulled a card holder from his shirt pocket, extracted a card, handed it to her and returned the holder to his pocket. "If I'm not at the top number, call the other two."

"Thank you again," she said.

He put the last of his tools into his tool bag. She led him to the front door. He walked out. After she closed it, she turned to lean against it.

"I don't know what to do," she said to her girlfriend who had been sitting at the kitchen table the whole time the doctor was in the apartment. "I just can't go off and leave him like this."

"Child, he's gonna get better with or without you. You got to do for yourself. He's got his own problems."

"I know, but he's worse off than I am."

"Don't let that stop you. I'll take care of him if he means that much to you."

A smile began to emerge from the gloominess of Bertha's face. "You're such a good friend. I don't know how my conscious will let you go out that far for me." Bertha went to sit at the table across from her.

Her girlfriend began to show signs of being disturbed as she watched Bertha. "Girl, I worked hard to get you into this Rehab. Center. If you don't go, I don't know how we will ever keep our friendship. Do you value our friendship stronger than you have with him?"

Bertha stared back. "You shouldn't ask such a question. You know that I do. We been friends every since I moved here. You will always be my friend no matter what."

"Then please, for my sake, go. Don't think about it. Do it for your children."

Bertha's face brightened up. "I will," she said sincerely.

For the next two days, the two gangs work together as if they were one. Every now and then a fight would breakout, but it ended in jokes and laughter.

Jesse and Flash managed to get enough drugs for all the members to take to the concert.

Flash fought down the urge to mug people and grab pocketbooks. He was starting to get along with the whole gang. A couple of times Flash said things that he later regretted, but he worked hard in trying to create his new image.

Sonny Bee stayed out of sight most of the time. Tenants continued to come sit on the bench in the courtyard while the police protection was visible. They sat around watching their children as they played. Most people stayed as far away from the parking lot as possible. None of the kids went near the sandbox. It had become a symbol of bad memories.

Tuesday morning, Bertha got up early. She and her boyfriend smoked a lot of crack in her bedroom. She was having such a good time, she changed her mind about going away.

Bertha's girlfriend came to her apartment around noon. When Bertha let her in, her girlfriend seen no change in things since the last time she was here. She stood in front of Bertha, trying to make eye contact, but

Bertha sort of held her head slightly down. There were no visible packed bags to be seen. Her girlfriend started to think the worse of things. "Do you want me to help you with your bags?"

"No, I'm not going. I changed my mind."

Her girlfriend looked shocked. "Bertha! Look at me." Bertha eased her head up slowly. "You been doing that stuff again, haven't you?" Bertha's voice had a very mild tone to it.

"Yeah, I thought I'd have one for the road," she smiled. "Then another and another." She was on a roll. She started to dance.

"Bertha!" her girlfriend called out calmly while fighting back the growing anger. Bertha stopped. "We still friends, right?"

Bertha went to the kitchen table to sit. Her girlfriend followed.

"We're the best," said Bertha.

"Prove it to me by going to the center."

"No, my boyfriend said…"

"Bertha, what kind of friends are we?"

Bertha's head seemed to straighten up with dignity. "We're the best."

"Lets get your things and go."

"Okay, if you say so."

"Anything packed?"

"My stuff's in the bedroom." Bertha rose from the table and headed toward the bedroom.

Her girlfriend followed but stopped short of the doorway.

Bertha walked across the room, passing her boyfriend as he lay on the bed with his eyes half closed. She opened her chest of drawers.

The sound caused him to fully open his eyes. He looked at her back. "What's up baby?' he asked softly.

She started packing selected items into a plastic grocery bag. "She talked me into going," her voice just barely audible.

His eyes widened. He wanted to talk loud but something within stopped him. "Them people ain't gonna do nothing for you."

"Go back to sleep," said her girlfriend. "You did enough already for today."

"Bertha, are you really gonna to leave me here like this? I'll be lonely without you."

Bertha stopped taking things from the drawer.

Her girlfriend walked toward the bed, looked down toward him with a disgusting look about her. "You wasn't lonely before you met her. I doubt if you'll be lonely when she's gone."

Bertha looked at him with tears in her eyes. "I got to go honey. God knows I got to go."

He made an attempt to remove himself from the bed, but his body was too weak to move. His face twisted in full pain.

"It's my only way back to a real way of life."

"But I thought we had this thing going?"

Bertha looked to her girlfriend. Her girlfriend shook her head from side to side. "We got to be there before 4 p.m."

Bertha walked to the bed, looked down at him. She couldn't resist giving him a tender kiss on the lips. He tried to move closer to her but she straightened up to blow him another kiss. Half dazed, she walked out bare handed. Her girlfriend lifted Bertha's clothing bag and moved to follow behind her.

He closed his eyes. Seconds later, the sound of a front door was heard opening and closing. He lay motionless. A breeze moved the still shades slightly to and from the open window.

The following morning, the reporter sat in the studio poring over his notes, waiting to go on the air. One of his female co-workers came to the table taking a seat next to him. He extended a warm smile to her as a gesture of hello. She casually smiled back and directed her attention to some papers of her own.

The silence of the room was broken by a voice starting to countdown through a miniature earphone attached to one of his ears. At an instant, another set of lights flashed on to brighten the area surrounding them. The voice through the earphone ended the count. A green light near the camera flashed on and the voice in his ear said, "You're on."

The reporter squeezed his loose papers together, looked toward the camera's direction, holding his head high with an expression of calmness that filled his face. He lifted one edge of the papers.

Words seemed to flow from his mouth smooth and evenly. "Today there is much unrest in Miller Homes. Half of all the Tenants have resorted to keeping their children indoors. They say gun fire can breakout at a moment's notice. Without around the clock police protection, this situation could last for a very long time.

"After dark, it gets even worse. No one can sleep because of dealers, buyers and thugs arguing about everything. Tenants say there is no end to buyers tooting horns at random. The drug operation goes on without outside interference. At times, there are so many transactions taken place in and around the parking lot that Tenants are afraid to drive near it for fear of their lives. A large majority of the Tenants want to move away, but most of them are on some type of government assistance that would make it impossible to do so at this present time.

"Recently, the Mayor informed me that lack of funding has limited his ability to hire more police officers to aide this troubled community against its drug war. But the Police Chief did say he brought back the two original patrolling officers plus four more from another area of the city.

"Only a small group of Tenants say they feel just little safer, while others say it's a slap in their face.

"The Miller Homes development is just one of the plaguing areas. The city is filled with troubled spots like this one. The Mayor had repeatedly put in request for the Governor to declare this city in a state of emergency but he has decline to act. In talking with the Police Chief, he tells me the jails are like an exchange program. For every wagon load that is delivered to the city jail, a wagon load is released because of over crowding. Dealers and thugs continue to run rampant in what they call their city. "Susan will have today's world news after this brief pause."

The camera focus moved back to expose Susan seated next to him.

Flash's Aunt turned off the television set. "Lordy be," she said in a whispering voice. "When I was a kid, we was always under strict hands. We got slapped for looking cross-eyes let alone doing stuff like that. And my poor brothers, I can see why they acted like angels. Them hard sticks can make soft behinds."

Flash walked from a spare bedroom into the kitchen smiling. "I couldn't picture you ever being a kid," jokingly he said. "You was born old." The sound of laughter rushed from his lips. She looked at his in amazement. "Don't lie," he continued, "Are you older than your mother?"

Understanding his poor mentality, she decided to laugh with him and in doing so, she recalled some memories of her own. "Don't be so smart. I remember your mother telling me when you was born, the doctor picked you up by your two feet. And when he tried to smack you on your little behind, you was so slippery, he dropped you on your head. We all thought you would grow up brain dead. And guess what?"

He bent over laughing so hard, water began flowing from his eyes. Finally, he straightened up, wiping his face with the back of his hands. "You always know the funniest things to say. I'd like to stay longer, but I got to finish getting ready for that bad concert they're having for school-aged kids."

"I guess you going, too. Ha?"

"Yeah, you know me. I like to be in on the in-things."

"Just stay out of trouble. You know how bad some of those kids are."

"Auntie. That's the least of my problems." He went back into the bedroom.

CHAPTER
Sixteen

The concert hall was located within the downtown area. A modern face looking building on the outside, occupying space equivalent to a whole city block. It sat back from the main street nearly two hundred and fifty feet and reaching four stories high.

The interior of the building needed lots of repairs. Sculptured ceiling and aging designed wallpaper showed signs of cracking. Depending on the type of event taking place, the structure held a capacity of six or so thousand seats.

On the day of the concert, the front of the building was mobbed with kids lining up on both sides of the building as far back as the corners trying to enter sectional doors leading inside for the special event. A limited number of police officers stood near the entrance trying to keep everyone orderly. Two additional officers stood in the street directing traffic into a drive thru area designed for dropping off people. Another single officer acted as a crossing guard, directed traffic near the building's front.

Store owners across the street watched as kids moved around outside their place of business, talking, joking and horse playing around. Most owners were glad to see kids going to something worthwhile other than hanging around streets causing trouble.

As soon as The Miller Homes' gang arrived, they immediately started walking through the line selling drugs with both hands. They worked between the building and massive lines to prevent detection from the police in the area.

The large mass thinned down into single lines as the kids inched their way toward the front door and through a turnstile. Just beyond the entrance stood a large, dark stained glass on an adjacent wall positioned to oversee individuals making their entrance.

Not more than fifteen feet beyond the dark stained glass stood a young white male dressed in sporty clothing with hair dangling beyond his shoulders. The tone of his voice was loud and bursting with energy. At times, he would retrieve small stacks of colored tickets from a long box with divided sections place directly before him. One by one, he'd passed a ticket to the on-coming stream of kids. "Hold onto your ticket," he shouted. "The color you're holding may determine if you get a prize and which one." They gladly grabbed a ticket. "Shame on you if your color's called and you missed getting your ticket." He rubbed a ticket on his arm before giving it to a young kid standing in front of him. "I'm giving you good luck Brother."

The boy looked at him seriously then started moving on. "I'm not your Brother," he replied in a high pitched voice.

"Check out your family tree. It's got colors in it just like the leaves on the trees in the fall.," said the ticket man. "You'll never know who's under those leaves." He picked up more tickets from the box and passed them to the oncoming continuous flow. "Don't forget your ticket. No seconds and no coming back."

The posse gathered a hundred feet from the outside entrance. Everyone was present except Flash. He promised to meet them at this location just before the show was about to start.

"Come on Jesse," said one of the members standing next to him. He showed signs of being highly emotionally disturbed. "We gonna miss the show. You know Flash ain't never on time."

"Give him a couple more minutes. I like checking out the chicks." His eyes widened when a young female crossed his front. She had a shape that Jesse thought was admirable. "Hey, sweet thing." He softly called out to her. "Can I sit next to you? We can talk about the first thing that pops up." He growled deeply while pretending to bite into his forearm.

She looked back and giggled. "I like animals. You wanna be my pet?"

The posse burst into a roar of laughter.

Jesse was all smiles. "Baby, I'll be your everything."

She disappeared into the loose crowd.

"Jesse! Quit messing around," shouted one angry member. "You can rap to them sugar babes later. We ready to split inside. We done sold all the drugs except for a little we saved for ourselves. It's after six. The show probably done started. Forget about Flash."

The posse started getting uneasy.

"I like the action out here better," said Jesse. "It's getting me high."

"You messing up really bad," said the first member.

Jesse tried to stare the member down. "Okay, lets slide inside. One of these days I'm gonna teach you dudes something about broads. They're the most beautiful creatures." When he kissed his fingers tips, the posse let out a roar of laughter.

"That's a bet!" Someone called out.

The whole posse walked to the front of the line. Jesse pushed a kid out of line, taking his spot and the posse lined up behind him. The kid rushed back to give Jesse a dirty look. Jesse balled his fist and held it close to the kid's face. "Is my presence causing you a problem?" asked Jesse.

The kid became calm. "No man. Take as much space as you need."

The ticket man was holding a bunch of orange tickets, still doing his thing when Jesse and his posse made their approach. He took notice of them. Quickly he placed the tickets back into their proper place and started to give Jesse one that is gray. "This might be your lucky day," he said eagerly.

"All I need is a couple of those fine chicks." The ticket man smiled. Jesse didn't like the color. "Give me one of those pink ones." He started reaching toward the box.

"No, no my good man," the ticket man responded in a low voice. "I got an inside tip that gray's gonna be the boss color."

"Is that so," Jesse responded curiously.

"Here, trust me." The man extended the ticket to Jesse.

"Okay, what do I have to loose?" Jesse took the ticket. Each of his members also took one of the same color.

"Enjoy the show," he called out as the posse walked away. The ticket man quickly returned the remaining gray tickets to their place in the box and this time grabbed a hand full of yellow tickets. Immediately began passing them out. "The hippest show in town." He began shouting. "Get your free tickets. Win a nice prize." His voice carried throughout the area.

    The posse walked through the outer portion of the auditorium. Sonny Bee was holding Sandy by the arm in an effort to keep her swaying body erect as they passed Jesse's posse heading in the opposite direction. Neither side spoke. By now, there were very few people walking around the outer area to the entertainment area. The posse made their way to a door leading into the auditorium. And as they filed inside the low lighted area, music flowed throughout the air in an up-beat tempo. Straight ahead of them, about two hundred feet was the stage. A male group had just finished performing and was in the middle of taking their bow before the emotionally, wild screaming crowd. The posse made their way half way down the middle aisle in mid-section to a row of half empty seats.

    A light skin male dressed in a dark suit and matching tie walked from behind stage to its center holding a wireless microphone. The performing group rushed off to one side of the stage and out of sight.

    "Give the Brothers another hand," he shouted and clapped. The crowd screamed louder while more kids came to their feet. Every member of the group reappeared. They bowled again and quickly rushed off stage for the last time. "I tell you," said the announcer.

"That's some bad group. Hey!" He switched the microphone from one hand to the other. "We got lots more entertainment to come. Brace yourself for more dynamite enjoyment." The lights came on. He placed one hand close to his eyes in an effort to protect them from the sudden burst of glaring light. "Man, these lights are a killer," he said while lowering his hand. "Are you having fun?" He screamed out at the crowd while holding the microphone out at arm's length.

"Yes!" Screamed the crowd.

He pulled the microphone back to his face and laughed slightly. "As you know, the entertainment will be running back to back J-U-S-T for you." He was interrupted by a loud burst of cheering. "But before." He stopped for a moment to wait for the cheering to die down. "But before we continue with the show, we want to make a few souls happy out there by giving away the prizes right now.

So." The noise grew louder. He put his hand up high for them to lower the noise. It took several seconds for the crowd to calm down to a point where he could continue to speak. "So, in case some of you might have to leave early, we wouldn't want the ticket holder to miss out on the prizes we have selected for you. Give us a few minutes to get the prizes on stage and arranged." He immediately proceeded to walk back stage as the curtain began to come down. The auditorium was just about filled mostly with kids of all ages. A member of the posse spotted Flash coming down the center aisle. Flash was punching a younger teen in the back and shoulder while talking wildly to him.

"Flash!" Jesse called out. "You big dummy, over here." Other member of the posse began to look around in search of Flash. As their eyes fell upon him, they began pointing to a seat they had saved for him.

Flash stopped punching and pushing the kid long enough to see the posse waving from the corner of his eye.

The boy whom Flash was attacking tried to move away, but Flash suddenly grabbed his arm. A thick line of kids moving quickly through the aisle almost forced Flash into a row of filled seats. He regained his stance by continuously holding onto the boy. The sudden pulling motion forced the boy to face Flash. Flash lifted a finger to stick into the boy's face and the boy slapped it away. Furiously, Flash started talking to him with evil pouring from his heart. The boy looked scared. Flash raised his fist, spat on its knuckles. The boy folded his arms around the top of his head. Feeling sorry for the boy, Flash pushed him away. The boy lost his balance but was quick to recover. Flash watched as he made his getaway. Contented that he had struck fear within his victim, Flash went to be with the posse, forcing his way to his seat by mashing toes along the way.

"I didn't think you was gonna show," said Jesse.

"Some days are like that. I had to deal with some punks who was holding out on me. Did I miss anything?"

"Nothing important."

The announcer returned to the stage. "Rather than spending almost an hour calling numbers during good show time, we're going to award prizes by ticket colors." The curtain went up. Another cheer came from the audience. Lots of prizes were on display, including those listed in the newspapers. "I sure wish I was sitting out there holding the right ticket," said the announcer excitingly.

A sea of different color tickets fanned the air above the audience's head as voices rang out confusingly wild. "Call red, white, orange, gray!"

The announcer held his hand high over his head. The whole room slightly became quieter. He pulled his hand down. "Listen carefully. As you can see, each of these prizes have a big tag on them. On the other side is a number. The number on each winning prize will match the number on your ticket. There should have been only one hundred of each color tickets passed out." He pulled an envelope from the inside of his jacket pocket and immediately began waving it high over his head. Shouting at the top of his voice, "I have the ticket color in here."

The crowd roared.

He pulled the envelope down and tore off one end. The crowd became quiet while he blew into it. Its sides parted. He held it out in front of him as a piece offering for more than a few seconds then pulled it back and flipped it over to release the contents into the other hand. He waved it back and forth over his head. "GRAY! The color is GRAY," he called out at the top of his lungs.

Loud cheers erupted from the audience along with louder boos.

"We all won something." A member of the posse shouted with pure delight. Other members realizing what just happened, joined in.

"Alright. Yeah." Several members started repeating the same words. Some stood on seats waving tickets and hands.

"Aright! Right on!" said the kid who had red about the concert in the newspaper. "I had that feeling I was gonna win."

"Me too," said another. "I even had dreams about winning. Yeah, the dude who gave us the tickets was right. That's my boy."

"Please hold your seat," said the announcer as he lowered the ticket. "Those with gray tickets, please move to the far left aisle. That's your left, not mine. Line up against the wall leading to the stage." The winners started moving toward the end aisle and lining up. "When you come on stage to find which prize you won, I'll give you a slip like this." He reached into his trouser back pocket and pulled out a small slip of white paper. He held it up high for all to see. "We have a room set up near the building's entrance with arrows pointing where to go to verify your prize."

Flash, Jesse and the remaining portion of the posse was among the first to get in line. Flash busied himself by fooling around with a few of the members, which ended up in light horse play. He was more excited than any of the others.

"Chill Flash!" Jesse called out angrily. "You mess around too much. Is this part of your new image?"

Flash didn't answer. He quickly calmed down and got in line.

The announcer watched as the winners continued to line up. He looked toward the audience. "All you gray ticket holders must get in line in order to receive your prize. After we get a count, the front and end of the line will be sealed off. No one, and I mean no one will be allowed to enter the line at that point."

Sonny Bee along with the few remaining kids went to join the selected winning few. He leaned against the wall looking into the audience. No smile, just the desire to receive something for free.

The announcer waved his hand above his head once again. "Can I have two officers at each end of the line? Four uniformed officers began moving into position.

"If I didn't know better, with all these Knight and this line up," said Jesse calmly, "you would think somebody was heading for the gray bar hotel." Laughter came from the posse.

The crowd began to get quiet. The Announcer motioned for someone behind the side stage curtain to come forth. "Mr. Walker will now take care of passing out the prizes.

A tall clean shaven man wearing a dark gray suit came to center stage. Several kids standing in line clapped. He spent several seconds looking over the audience. "I'm deeply honored to present these prizes to our young generation along with the show. For years, this city has wanted to do something special for our youth. To show how much we care about you. After all, you represent our future," he smiled. "For some of you, this might be your bluest day yet, but be thankful today we have more winners than losers." He looked over the audience, finally bringing his eyes to rest on the line standing along the wall. He held his hand high above his head. The plain clothes officers seated along the two left end seats nearest the line rose. Upon drawing their pistol, they aimed them in the direction of the winners.

Some of the kids were quick to jump with their back against the wall out of fear for their lives. All types of sounds came from the lined up winners. Mr. Wilson continued to stare at the winners. "If any of you winners dare to reach into your pockets, these officers have permission to shoot you deader than a door knob." He turned his attention to the audience. "As for everyone else, please. I advise you to kindly remain in your seat. This is a Sting Operation. We are only after the people lined against the wall. Please let us take care of this little matter as quickly as possible. Thank you for your cooperation."

Kids in their seat nearest the action began to move away to anywhere they could put distance between their seat and the Sting Operation.

Mr. Wilson stood ready to give commands. "Everyone standing near the wall, turn to face the wall. My warning is still my best advice. Don't try the officers."

The first row of officers nearest the aisle moved into place and began handcuffing winners while the next row of officers trained their pistol to cover the line. The officers searched each winner. Weapons and drugs were recovered. Most of the weapons came from Jesse's posse as well as a limited quantity of drugs.

The audience remained tense, anticipating gun fire to breakout. Mr. Walker gave the microphone back to the announcer.

"The show will continue in a few minutes," he said eagerly. "Please be patient. We are sorry to have you witness this. This is our only way to help put an end to a growing problem." The curtain came down. "You may know these people standing along the wall. This is what happens to drug dealers and people who choose to commit crimes. Don't end up like this bunch. These kids may have already destroyed their future. Avoid drugs. Avoid street gangs. Listen to your parents. Try to do things that make sense and seek help when in doubt. As long as you have freedom, you're a winner. And now let's get on with the show. Give a big hand for the Jive four."

The crowd cheered wildly.

After the last juvenile had been handcuffed, Mr. Wilson came down the side steps into the aisle where the line had formed. He walked past everyone heading toward the front while looking back at his collection of winners. He had them face him. With a wave of his hand, he led the train out of the auditorium to waiting patrol wagons in front of the building. The handcuffed group no longer fearing for their lives, laughed and joked as they moved along.

"So you dudes want to be winner," Jesse's words were filled with laughter.

"Damn," said Flash, "I wasn't late after all. But I did wanna see the Jive Four. They can really jam."

Upon reaching the wagons, the group was stopped and counted into groups of tens. Another officer moved them forward and helped them climb into the wagons.

Jesse, Flash and Sonny Bee sat quietly in the patrol wagon while two officers stood next to the opened door.

The undercover officer walked to the wagon's rear with his arm and shoulder partly bandaged. He stood directly in front of the opened door looking inside. "I got you," was his shocking words to the group.

Flash looked up when he heard the officer's voice and jumped in his seat as if seeing a ghost. The other two, who were sitting with their eyes closed, looked to see what was going on. Jesse stared at the officer. Sonny Bee dropped his head to his knees.

"Where did you come from?" asked Flash.

"From behind that dark glass. The one nearest the front door you had to pass in order to get in."

"I knew there was something queer about you," said Jesse. "You're a undercover Knight. I should have known from day one since you're not from around here. Don't you ever show your face around here again. Ever."

"Where you're going, you won't have to worry about being around here either." The officer looked directly at Flash. "You big dummy. You caused me a lot of unnecessary grief. I wanted you so bad, I told the ticket holder to give you two tickets, but Boss Man said one was enough. He thought by giving you two, you would have thought something was up and probably left. I told him he was wrong. You wanted it all."

Flash seemed impatient in asking a question. "You mean this whole thing was a set up?"

"Did you hear the man use the word, Sting?"

Flash opened his mouth, but didn't say a word.

"A group of us was standing behind the glass talking to the guy passing out the tickets. He was wired up real nice. That's how he knew to make sure you was included."

"I should of known," said Jesse. "That's why I couldn't get a pink ticket."

The officer looked at Jesse. "I could even see your posse selling drugs along the sidewalk. We took some pictures."

Jesse lowered his head. A couple kids were brought to completely fill the wagon. Jesse, Flash and Sonny Bee found themselves squeezed together like sardines in a can. The undercover officer walked away and another uniformed officer came to the rear to read them their rights. When he had finished, the doors were closed and locked. Seconds later, the wagon was driven away.

Special arraignments was awaiting the arrested group when taken to the county courthouse. As the patrol wagons arrived, the groups were unloaded under police escort and rushed into and awaiting courtroom.

Everyone was able to fit inside. A presiding Judge sat behind his bench looking down at the group before him still in handcuffs. Several unarmed officers stood throughout the court room.

The group began to chatter.

"Quiet," shouted the Judge in a stern voice. "This is my courtroom. You're in my house now. Do you understand that?" The room became quiet. "Is there anyone having trouble understanding why you are here?"

Unable to raise their cuffed hands, most of them answered. "No."

"Have all these kids been red their rights?" The Judge asked.

"Yes your Honor," answered an officer. "I went around to each wagon and personally red to all of them myself."

The Judge leaned forward enough in his chair to almost place his chest against his desk. He stared at the group. "I don't understand you kids for the life of me. You had everything in the world going for you. And what do you do? You chose to sell drugs and do criminal acts against the law. Do any of you realize what effects you're having on that society outside this courthouse? Do you know how many years you could possibly receive from this courthouse?" The group continued to remain silent. "I know most of you have been out there a long time doing your thing. This is the end of the line. IT'S OVER. Let that sink in." The Judge pointed to a stack of papers next to his arm. "All these papers have your names on them. You're a selected group. These are warrants for each and every one of your arrest. I'm setting bail at $50,000 for each of you with no ten percent. Think about that while you're sitting in your cell. Officers, take them away." The Judge stood and walked to a side door not far from his seat. He pushed it inward and moved out of sight. All arrestees were returned to waiting patrol wagons. Females were placed together in a separate wagon. The wagons finally rolled away one at a time into the street traffic.

Three at a time, the wagons pulled into the county jail's detention drop off area. One by one the wagons back doors were opened and passengers filed out. They were led up a back stairway leading to an empty tier that had been cleared just for them. The waiting officers started filling cells from front to rear. By two's, they were escorted to their new home. As the pairs were locked in, they began to laugh at others passing after them. At first they thought it was funny, but as the line neared its end, everyone began to quiet down. Reality was starting to set in about their state of condition. The freedom to come and go, as well as the freedom to see the outside world had all been eliminated from their lives. Their world was beginning to transform into a new way of life.

It was afternoon, the opening sound of a cell block gate broke the silence. Two inmates pushing a large food cart filled with trays made their way into the cell block area. After reaching the first cell, one inmate continued pushing the cart while the other pushed trays of food through a slotted opening on each cell door.

Sonny Bee was in the fourth cell sitting on his unmade bunk when a tray was placed in his slot. He went to where the tray was. Looking it over and stirring his finger around in it, he began to complain. "I can't eat garbage looking like this." He pushed the tray back through the slot. It made a clanging sound as the metal tray emptied its contents onto the concrete floor. "Send mine to the pig farm," he said.

"Give that royal punk a steak and baked potato," shouted Flash. The sound of laughter immediately filled the air.

An officer came into the cell block taking names of each person in each cell.

Meanwhile, the inmates continued talking. "You got royalty alright," a different voice called out. "And you're a darling of a winner, too."

Laughter filled the cell block.

"Who said that?" shouted Sonny Bee. "I'm gonna do something to you when I get a chance."

"You couldn't bust a grape. You better be glad you're in that cell. If you was over here with me, there'd be sweet dreams."

"Alright," Jesse shouted. "Cool it. We got enough problems."

A few guys pushed their trays back through the slot of their cell. More food splashed over the floor. One inmate who was passing out trays came back to clean up the mess.

The officer taking names observed the action. He went to one of the cells. "Next time you try that you won't be eating in this hotel for as long as you're taking up space. The choice is yours. And that goes for every one of you clowns."

From the other end of the cell block someone called out. "Why don't you sneak back to where you came from".

The officer ignored the remark and went back to taking names.

Because the group arrested was so large, it took several hours to get all the paper work in order. Finally, the processing got underway. In groups of four, the kids were taken for I.D.'s and questioning. Sonny Bee and his cell partner, along with those in the next cell were being taken to the ground floor by elevator. It seemed a long slow ride. Suddenly the elevator stopped. Two officers, one in the front and the other following moved them along a narrow hallway. They arrived at a small area where several officers were working at their desk. The three inmates accompanying Sonny Bee was led to seats along the wall. Sonny Bee was taken up to the desk and seated. An officer on the other side looked up from a folder he held. "So you're Sonny Bee," he said in a smart way. "The dude with the fancy car."

Sonny Bee smiled slightly. "Yeah, that's me."

The officer's face took on a stern composure. "Is that a big B or a little b?"

Sonny Bee looked confused. "What you talking about?"

"Big boy or little boy? Sonny B-O-Y."

Sonny Bee became angered. His face began to glow. "Was you Mother a boy?"

The officer jumped up from his seat. Another officer standing beside him grabbed his arm. "Don't let these punks get under your skin."

Sonny Bee shouted in anger. "Who you calling a punk? You're a punk yourself."

The office holding the officer's arm behind the desk let go. He started toward Sonny Bee. The officer behind the desk grabbed his arm. "You're right. Don't let him get under your skin." He let the officer go. They straighten their clothes. The officer behind the desk stared at Sonny Bee for a couple of seconds before returning to his seat. The other officer moved back to where he was standing.

Sonny Bee stared back at the seated officer. The officer pointed his finger toward Sonny Bee's face. "When they come around for sick call, you better tell them to give you a face repair kit and a new set of upper and lower teeth. In the morning you gonna need them."

Sonny Bee smiled. "Yes sir. Have them sent to your Momma. That old bag."

With those words, the officer behind the desk tried to grab Sonny Bee, but he moved out of reach. The other officer rushed in to remove Sonny Bee from the room.

Sonny Bee started shouting as he was being pulled away by his arm. "That old bag will probably enjoy them more in the morning than I ever will."

"I'll see you later," shouted the officer.

Everyone in the office had been watching since the first outburst. The next kid was taken up to the desk. He looked scared.

The officer behind the desk stared at him. "Sit down," said the officer viscously. The kid didn't move. "Do I have to knock you down?" The kid obeyed. The officer pointed his finger straight at the kid. "Don't even try what he just did. Kid or not." The room remained quiet while the officer took his seat.

Two days later, some of the kids began talking as part of a plea bargaining agreement. During the bargaining sessions, it was brought out that Bertha's boyfriend was still holding out in her apartment. Three officers were sent to Bertha's apartment. They broke down the door, charged inside and arrested him without a fight. He believed Bertha had sold him out, thinking she had wanted to be rid of him. He sent her a letter from jail saying he would get even with her the next time they meet.

Several other drug dealers and thugs were also rounded up. This sudden example of enforcing the law scared some of the other dealers and thugs into leaving the area.

CHAPTER Seventeen

Six months later, the Mayor received funding for his Miller Homes programs. On Tower One's first floor, the SAY NO TASK FORCE set up an office manned by police officers. It was the beginning of the end for the once popular drug haven. This task force taught kids how to identify various drugs through sight and the various ways they were packaged. They were also taught about the dangerous side effects drugs caused and also how to report what they saw to parents and authorities. Movies and slides were being shown on a monthly basis to further educate those interested in protection their community.

A raw iron fence was constructed around the entire Miller Homes' perimeter with several entrances. A roving patrol of two officers made rounds day and night throughout the Towers and across the grounds. Still there was some drug activities, but it was so small that any person who saw it would have to think twice and still wonder about what they saw.

The sand box was removed. Two large gym sets were provided for kids as a replacement.

For once in as many years, people could remember, peace was established again within Miller homes. More people came outside to sit on benches to enjoy the fresh air and the sound of children playing.

Bertha recovered from her drug addiction. The six-month ordeal in Rehab. was a lot harder than she could ever imagine. When she first entered the program, she fought constantly in her mind everyday with determination to recover. She didn't want to return to the empty life left behind. No visitors were allowed at the Center. The administration believed visitors often brought bad news and sometimes had a tendency to influence patients in the wrong direction. This was a leading cause in slowing down the rehabilitation process.

Bertha was allowed to receive mail. At times she received family mail from down south telling her how Breeze was doing. Breeze had become an honor roll school student and was making plans to do wonderful things with his life. She enjoyed reading this kind of news. It often made her happy. She also received letters from her girlfriend. One letter informed her about the Sting Operation and another about her boyfriend's removal from her apartment. Bertha had already red about it in the newspaper. It made her sad to learn that her apartment had been rented to someone else. In a way, this was good. Going back to the same old neighborhood would certainly encourage her to activate some of her old habits and practices.

Today she was checking out, heading for a new start at life. During her stay at the Rehab. Center, she was trained to be a Secretarial Assistant and File Clerk. She made high scores on all her test. They were so good, a large Corporation offered her a job but she turned it down. There were other things she wanted to pursue. She had neglected her kids before going to the Center. Things would be different this time. She decided it was time to get her daughter and the both of them would go down south to live with her son. She was going to be someone both her kids could be proud of. In the past, she had demonstrated a lot of wrong doing with her kids. It led them to thinking in the wrong direction she was leading them. But now that she had had these months to think things out, she was ready to do the right thing.

She walked out of the building. Took a deep breath of fresh air. It felt good. Her immediate thoughts were those of Miller Homes. She knew those days were over but for old time sake, she would return just to picture the memories of good and bad times.

She hailed a taxi. Had the driver take her to Miller Homes. Along the way, she remembered things that had happened to her at various locations. The taxi pulled into the parking lot next to the fence. She sat gazing out the window. Miller Homes seemed like a different place. No crowds in the parking lot. Graffiti missing from Towers. Lots of new windows in place. Even grass was starting to cover barren spots. And kids playing on the gym sets without parental guidance.

She stepped from the taxi. Stood staring at the high rise Tower where for years she called home. She looked up toward the window that use to be her apartment and walked up close to the fence, sticking her fingers through its holes. She continued to stand stationary. Thoughts raced through her mind in wonderment of the people now living up there. Are they enjoying her apartment and the view of the area along with the neighboring friends as much as she did?

Bertha looked around at the people sitting on benches. It's a shame how people get caught up into spending a lot of their best years doing nothing constructive with their life. Her girlfriend had been the champion of friends to have pushed her out of this stagnant spot knowing she, herself may never break free.

Bertha released the fence. This would not be the right time to go visit her girlfriend. She would write to her when she arrived down south to give thanks for all the years of dedicated friendship. A tear trickled down the side of her face. She walked back to the taxi and returned to her seat. She held her head down as the taxi carried her away. An officer standing outside a little booth watched as the taxi road out of sight. A long list of memories was all she took with her.

During the past several months, bail was deduced for many of those arrested. Most of those released, gave confessions about their activities in the posse and provided information about others involved.

Bail for Jesse, Sonny Bee and Flash was increased to one million dollars each. All of Sonny Bee's possessions were confiscated by the court, including his Jaguar and the lease on his apartment was terminated due to lack of payment. Sonny Bee confessed to being involved in the shootout with Flash and the posse at the time when the baby was killed. He also confessed to being the ring leader and a major drug supplier for the posse in exchange for a possible lighter sentence.

Flash never confessed to anything. Bullets extracted from Butch's body matched those from his gun. Several people pointed him out as the person who had robbed them. One thing came as no surprise to Flash. Evidence pointed to him as being a dangerous and cold blooded murderer in the case of the six plain clothes officers killed.

Pictures taken from the Sting Operation caught Jesse and several members in the act of dealing drugs to minors. These were collected along with numerous weapons. However, no one was ever charged with the baby's death. No witnesses came forth and the bullet that had been fired went through the baby's body and never found. Word had gotten out that the three were up for heavy numbers.

On the third day of their trial, Sonny Bee, Jesse and flash appeared together in court. The Judge sat behind his bench looking down at the three. They stood at attention. The room was silent. Their three appointed lawyers sat behind a long wooden table whispering amongst themselves.

"Can I have your attention," asked the Judge. The three lawyers stood and looked toward the Judge. "For three days, I have heard witnesses and related facts. From the information I have gathered, it appears that this society has no place for any of the three prisoners.

"Flash, it amazes me how one person such as yourself, not yet an adult has left such a devastating effect on the Miller Homes Community. You, Sonny Bee, the oldest in the group. I guess there's no limit to a person's desire for wealth. You used the youth of your community to prosper and advance your own status. Those kids you used will carry a bad mark against them throughout the rest of their life.

"Jesse, a so call man with a thirst for power. A conniver and shrewd manipulator. I must admit I am surprised by the way you took over Sonny Bee's gang to join up with you so you could become King of the Mountain. If I had my way, none of you would ever see the streets again. But that's for the Jury to decide.

"I want to make it clear that those people living in Miller Homes are entitled to the respect, dignity and safety that every American is entitled to without fear and reprisal. People like you three disrupt other's lives, take away children's values and create problems for the Community as a whole.

"The Jury has already decided that all three of you are guilty. Tomorrow will bring the decision for each one of your faith. Sheriff, remove the prisoners."

The court appointed Lawyers followed them out of the courtroom.

CHAPTER Eighteen

The new beginning

On the south side of the City, in a rundown neighborhood, a young man sits parked across the street in his new BMW watching three of his teenage drug dealers hustling drugs with passer-buyers. The sight of little bags being exchanged for folded cash brings a smile to his face behind the dark sun glasses and black felt hat he wears.

THE END

CONCLUSIONS

Miller Homes had completely deteriorated into a state of unhealthiness. Dogs were used to help rid rats from hallways in the high rise, while roaches had accumulated to such proportion they began feasting on flies clinging to apartment ceilings as a means of survival.

During the early years of the 1990's, City Council forced every resident in Miller Homes to relocate. Plans for renovations have been set forth to once again make Miller Homes the pride of new achievements.

Beginning around the year 2000, the City made a decision that the Two Towers were beyond repair. And so a demolishing company was hired to demolish both Towers. But it didn't happen.

As for existing single unit homes, they have never been in major disrepair. The City was able to refurbish them and now they are being well kept by Tenants who reside within them.

ABOUT THE AUTHOR

Charles Feggans lived all of his younger and teenage years in cities such as Philadelphia, Pennsylvania and Trenton, New Jersey. After leaving the military, he returned to Trenton, New Jersey where he experienced life living in a community where people were bunched up together in a warehousing like setting. Being slightly poor, he saw the ins and outs of daily life where people had just enough to live on. He saw gangs who live and hung around different high and low housing developments. He saw the drug dealers who created an open market and the gangs who disrespected people they though were an easy target. He saw elderly people living in a simple life style who just wanted to live out the rest of their lives peacefully. He thought about writing this book as a way of letting readers know that there is another side to life if you have never lived in government housing.

www.ingramcontent.com/pod-product-compliance
Lightning Source LLC
LaVergne TN
LVHW041224080526
838199LV00083B/2490